PRAISE FOR *THE PROPRIETOR'S SONG*

"Loved this. What a great read and respite from poetry."

— Dorianne Laux, finalist for the 2020 Pulitzer Prize

"Janet Goldberg writes so powerfully of loss and grief. We follow the crooked paths of people left stumbling behind those who have gone on (a son, a sister) until we recognize our own intimate irresolvable journey in theirs. The author manages to say the unsayable. A truly original and effervescent writer."

— Stephanie Cowell, American Book Award recipient, author of *Claude & Camille* and *The Boy in the Rain*

"Goldberg's poetic descriptions of Death Valley, its alluring and treacherous landscape, set the tone for *The Proprietor's Song*, a subtle novel about grief, mortality, hope, and despair."

— Fredrick Soukup, author of *Bliss* and *Blood Up North*

THE PROPRIETOR'S SONG

Janet Goldberg

Regal House Publishing

Published by
Regal House Publishing, LLC
Raleigh, NC 27605
All rights reserved

ISBN -13 (paperback): 9781646033553
ISBN -13 (epub): 9781646033560
Library of Congress Control Number: 2022943728

All efforts were made to determine the copyright holders and obtain their permissions in any circumstance where copyrighted material was used. The publisher apologizes if any errors were made during this process, or if any omissions occurred. If noted, please contact the publisher and all efforts will be made to incorporate permissions in future editions.

Cover images and design by © C. B. Royal

Lyrics from "The Journey" by James Wright used by permission of Annie Wright.
"Hallelujah" by Leonard Cohen, collected in *Stranger Music: Selected Poems and Songs.* © 1993 Leonard Cohen and Leonard Cohen Stranger Music, Inc., used by permission of The Wiley Agency LLC.

Regal House Publishing, LLC
https://regalhousepublishing.com

Printed in the United States of America

For Debbie & Alex

We came unto a place where loud the pilot
Cried out to us, "Debark, here is the entrance."
More than a thousand at the gates I saw
Out of the Heavens rained down, who angrily
Were saying, "Who is this that without death
Goes through the kingdom of the people dead?"

—Dante

1

From northern California there are various routes to Death Valley. One of the more direct, less scenic routes involves a tedious drive down I-5 through the flat San Joaquin Valley and Bakersfield, a hot, dry suburban sprawl of fast food, gas stations, and shopping centers. Once out of Bakersfield, the drive gets better. The road gains elevation as it cuts through the Tehachapi Mountains where even a late spring snow can dust everything white before descending down into the hot flats of Ridgecrest, a military town where young mothers tote bawling children in triple digit heat, where dead dogs, some in full rigor on their backs, legs sticking up, are pushed off to the side of the road. Ridgecrest, the gateway to Death Valley.

Next comes Trona, the last town before scrappy desert takes over, and Trona, compared to Ridgecrest, seems a virtual ghost town. Its main occupant, a chemical plant, looms over the desolate town like a giant spider from a bad science fiction movie belching chalky, acrid gas. Dwarfed by the plant are small roads populated by shacks, rusted-out trailers, and boarded-up businesses. Oddly enough, Trona has a brand-new bicycle lane, its lines painted golden yellow, yet there are no bikes or no one riding them. In fact, in Trona, there's little sign of life, except for the chemical plant's truck-filled lot and the road's few moving cars, most on their way somewhere else having briefly detoured out to Trona's Pinnacles, a bizarre set of rocky protrusions, fins they call them, where supposedly *Planet of the Apes* was filmed. The only other notable landmark is the Trona rest area, where a surprisingly clean cinderblock restroom sits on a small lot alongside a picnic table, and a nice breeze blows if you don't mind inhaling the acrid breath of the spider.

Three years ago, this was the very route Jared Fisher had

told his parents he and his college roommates were taking
into Death Valley over spring break, but as it turned out the
boys had taken a different route, through the Sierras and Lake
Tahoe's dark forests, over to Bridgeport, a small eastern Sierra
town, where they'd stayed overnight, then down to Mono Lake
and the Owens Valley, and over finally to the desert. Had Jared
Fisher come back from Death Valley, as the other boys had,
none of this would have mattered to his parents Grace and Elwood. Living up in northern California, across the bay from San
Francisco, they themselves had never strayed into the desert, so
they'd just wanted their son to be careful. They'd worried about
his car, an old Cougar he'd fixed up himself, breaking down or
them driving too long, falling asleep behind the wheel, some big
rig plowing into them. What they didn't worry about was their
son disappearing in the middle of nowhere, in Death Valley's
backcountry, at a place they'd never heard of—the Racetrack
Playa—and what they hadn't planned on was retracing their
son's tracks each spring, this their third, driving the same route
in, stopping on their way up, as their son had, at 6,500 feet in
Bridgeport to overnight at the Sleepy River Lodge and then
traveling the second leg of the trip the next day into Death
Valley, to the Furnace Creek Ranch, the last place their son had
been seen alive.

In the motel office Stanley Uribe was tapping his pencil on the
counter, wondering where the Fishers were. It was dark out,
around 9:00 p.m., and he was tired. Once again at their request,
he'd blocked off room 121, the very room their son and his
friends had stayed before he'd disappeared. What they expected to find there he didn't know, the room having been slept
in so many times since, and though their son's disappearance
had brought attention to Bridgeport and his motel—reporters
from *The San Francisco Chronicle* and *L.A. Times* had stayed with
him—the story had long died down, the flyers of their missing
boy having disintegrated winters ago or been torn down, replaced with others not because the town was rife with crime or

kidnappings—it was rife with fishermen and deer hunters—or anything else of interest for that matter but because, as Stanley knew well, even the missing fell by the wayside. *Letting go, acceptance, moving on* was the recommended trajectory. He knew this because six months ago his own sister Lorna had been found dead, and no one could tell him why. And now he thought he understood what the Fishers had been going through, even though their cases differed, and they likely only knew him as the man from the motel where their son had stayed shortly before disappearing.

Headlights flashed through the front window. Stanley put his pencil down and looked up. A car was pulling in, the Fishers he assumed, but then he saw it was Sheriff Boyd, the sheriff who'd questioned him right after the Fisher boy's disappearance and was handling Lorna's case and had been stopping in time to time for a friendly cup of coffee. Since the sheriff's department was treating her death as suspicious, Stanley still knew very little about what had happened, except that there was no evidence of foul play. But that, however, didn't mean there wasn't foul play, as Sheriff Boyd had said early in the investigation, a kind of doublespeak he was still getting used to.

"Evening Stanley." Sheriff Boyd poured some coffee, then stuck a stir straw in, stirring it up, even though he drank it black. "Open late tonight."

"Waiting on the Fishers."

The sheriff looked over the brim of his cup. "The Fishers? As in Jared Fisher?"

"Asked for the same room again. Guess they think he's still alive. Why they keep coming up here."

Sheriff Boyd shrugged. "Found people gone longer. Course not all of them wanted rescue. But I don't think that's the case here."

"So not a runaway?"

"Doesn't fit the profile—middle aged, bad marriage, debt. Those are the folks that go off the radar. Kids do too of course, but the Racetrack Playa would be a hell of a place to go. Why go all the way out there? Where would you run to? Nothing for miles. Doesn't make sense. Plus, as I recall, the Fishers seem like good people." He poured more coffee. "Anyway, it's not Jared Fisher I'm here about. It's your sister."

"You mean I'm no longer a person of interest?"

"Like I told you, in cases like this everybody's a person of interest."

"So you know what happened?"

"Not exactly. Coroner's still working on that. You know, more tests—blood and tissue they took before they released her. To be sent out." He slid an envelope toward Stanley. "But the preliminary autopsy report is in, and it's yours to read if you think you can stomach it. It might not make sense to you, all the jargon and such, but it's something."

Stanley peered down at the white envelope—ordinary, business size, Inyo County Coroner's Office stamped at the top left—and sucked in his breath, the first concrete thing since Lorna had died. How many times had he called the coroner's office right afterward asking if she was really there, if there'd been a mistake, and after a long pause always the same terrible answer and still he couldn't believe it.

"Came back clean," Sheriff Boyd said. "No cause of death. Unremarkable. Happens sometimes. But there's more that's not in the report if you want to know. Not everybody does."

Stanley looked up.

"How she was found. In her pajamas, on her bed, facedown, her boy Dell trying to wake her up. Said she was cold and stiff. Said she'd thrown up. But I think her boy knew right away."

"Knew what—that she died in her sleep?"

"Your sister was found facedown *across* the bed. On top of the blankets. No one sleeps like that."

"So what are you saying?"

"I'm not saying anything. In fact, I've probably said too much. And I can't say anymore. Not until the coroner concludes his investigation. That's the problem with information. It doesn't always make things clearer. Now I'm sorry to ask again but you're sure she wasn't depressed, nothing scaring her? Anything you haven't told us?"

Stanley shook his head, though he hadn't been completely truthful—lots scared Lorna, but she wouldn't have liked him telling on her, and he didn't want them thinking she'd killed herself or something like that, even though more than anything else he wanted it to be over, to end.

"Stanley?"

"I don't know anyone who'd want to hurt her. And there were no signs of foul play, right? So why do you keep asking?"

"She wasn't dating anyone?"

"Not that I know of, not since she and Ray, her ex, split. You must have gone through her things. Talked to him."

"And before the split?"

"She wasn't that kind of person. My sister was quiet, unassuming. She had her faults like everyone else."

"Like what?"

"I don't see why that matters anymore."

"Now, Stanley, it's no sin to speak ill of the dead. It's like you said—we all have faults."

Stanley sighed and rubbed his face. "Okay. Look, Lorna could be rigid. She had a strong sense of right and wrong, was very devoted to my father, took care of him as best she could when the Alzheimer's began, and after he went into the nursing home she'd get mad if I didn't see him often enough. She liked to control things."

"So she's not so quiet and unassuming."

"She was—most of the time. That's what I mean. People aren't all one thing. Why pick her apart? It's bad enough."

"What kind of relationship did you have with her? Would she have told you if she was in trouble?"

Stanley put his hand on the envelope and pulled it toward him. "She was a good person. She didn't deserve to die like that. Alone. By herself. She would have been terrified." He shook his head; he felt his eyes well up, but he swallowed hard.

"Now there's no use tormenting yourself about that. Doubt that's what Lorna would have wanted." He tossed his cup in the garbage. "But don't worry, we'll find an answer. I feel confident about this one. The Fisher boy though…" He glanced out to the parking lot. "In the meantime take care of yourself, Stanley. You look awful. Live."

"Live?"

"While you're alive. Many thanks for the coffee."

As he watched Sheriff Boyd pull out of the lot, he pondered the advice. He knew tragedy was supposed to ignite newfound appreciation for life, but when the call had come in, ending with the requisite *I'm sorry for your loss*—how many times had he heard that—he'd slipped down the rabbit hole, and he knew joining a bunch of sympathetic people sitting around in a circle weeping wouldn't help him out of it. Finding out what had happened would, but the wait was excruciating and what if, despite Sheriff Boyd's confidence, he'd have to live like the Fishers, never knowing? *Facedown. Across the bed.* What *had* made him think she'd died in her sleep? He turned the envelope over, slipped his finger beneath the flap, and pulled the autopsy report out. It should have made him feel better, but then he felt a sharp slicing pain, a thin line of blood, and lifted his finger to his mouth. He walked back into his quarters, ran some water over it, then covered it with a Band-Aid, and returned to the office. He looked out to the parking lot, then at his watch, realizing he'd almost forgotten about the Fishers. Where were they? Long stretches of 395 were poorly lit. Trucks drove the route, barreling down, the margin of error small. Or maybe the Fishers had decided to cancel, do a no-show, having moved on to *acceptance.* He looked back down at the envelope, dots of dried blood on the flap. He turned to his key rack and pulled 121, fingering its notches—river view, two queens, a bonus room with a fold-out couch, a funky wooden bar with a small fridge beneath, much too large for a couple. Then he opened a drawer pulling out a faded yellow registration card, the handwriting on it not his own rushed scrawl but the Fisher boy's, all capitals slanting slightly right: *JARED FISHER. COUGAR. 1969. PURPLE. CA 66A59JU.* He'd held on to it, pulling it out every so often on slow nights. But other than the handwriting, there'd been nothing unusual about the boy. Had he and his friends started trouble, he probably would have remembered him better. It was the louts—door swinging open, some guy in boxer shorts, cigarette hanging out of his mouth, TV blaring, kids out the sliding door feeding the cute raccoons and their babies—you remembered. Come winter, the babies separated from their mothers, they'd starve, not knowing how to forage. Those folks you remembered. The self-absorbed, ignorant, well-intentioned killers.

He put the card down, kept his eyes on the dark window, half expecting the Fisher boy's lone figure to pass by, crazy as it was, knocking on the window, bearded and haggard, saying, "Hey, it's me. Remember me? I'm alive," just as he'd imagined Lorna appearing, her hair swinging, a casual smile of victory on her face, her death an elaborate joke, and then the waiting would be over. He slid the autopsy report back in the envelope and turned his eyes upward to the deer mounted on the wall opposite him, there when he'd bought the place. Except for the eyes, it looked real enough, and he had no reason to doubt it was, venison on every menu up here. Maybe that's why his wife Caitlin, a vegetarian and ER nurse, had left him when he'd first proposed moving out of Sonora—a touristy, foothill town where they'd both grown up—up to Bridgeport, population 110.

He checked the time again. 9:30 p.m. That meant all of the restaurants would be closed, except for Miguel's up the street. If the Fishers didn't arrive soon, they'd go hungry. Stanley picked up the phone. Maybe he could catch Miguel before he cleaned up the kitchen. But just as the line rang, he saw headlights again. He hung up, slid the registration card back in the drawer. He'd planned to hand it over this time, but he didn't want the Fishers thinking he'd been waiting for them, even though that was his job, waiting for people to arrive, then making sure they left. Soon the car engine would go silent, the office door open, the bell jangling, and then the sound of footsteps, perhaps a cough or a clearing of the throat—the proprietor's song he called it, how people arrived and left.

"Good evening, Mr. Fisher," Stanley said.

Elwood smiled wanly and reached behind for his wallet. "Sure is cold out."

Face slack, eyes red-rimmed, he looked tired, Stanley thought, but his hair, a dull, yellowish blond, combed over, was no different, and he was just as bearish in body, mourning not wasting him away. Stanley pulled up the room reservation. "Everything okay? You're a little later than expected." He glanced out the door toward the car. "Mrs. Fisher okay?" He saw the passenger door opening, dark, stick-like legs swinging out.

"Long drive, that's all." Elwood's eyes roved around the room.

Stanley handed him a blank registration card to fill out, though he didn't need it anymore, computerized now, but he liked going through the motions, having handwriting on paper, evidence of life.

The door opened again, and the bell jangled.

"Good evening, Mrs. Fisher," Stanley said. "Coffee's still hot." He gestured toward the table. She was blond too but a darker shade and wavy, lots of it pinned up like a fountain on her head, and she was still very thin, like timber, older-looking, but with a pretty face, green eyes, and a pleasant smile, two rows of perfect teeth. "Oh, I almost forgot," Stanley said. "You must be hungry and it's late." He lifted the phone.

"That's all right," Elwood said, "we ate on the way up this time." He pushed the registration card forward. "We just need some sleep."

Stanley turned back to his board and pulled a duplicate of 121.

"They don't live very long, do they?" Grace said. She nodded toward the open door behind him, to his living quarters. "Your angels back there. In the tank."

"Well, they live long enough if you take care of them, the temperature and the PH balance," Stanley said, peering through the entryway into his living room. He pushed the key toward Mr. Fisher. "Sure you don't want to stay two nights? There's a ghost town down the road, an old gold mining settlement the park district just restored. Antelope run wild there."

"Antelope?" Elwood said. "Like deer?" He turned and looked up at the deer.

"Bigger and meaner, though sometimes they're hard to tell apart," Stanley said. "Best seen from the car unless you're a hunter."

Elwood raised his eyebrows. "Hmm. I didn't know deer were mean. Ours eat the roses right off our bushes."

"Did you shoot it?" Grace was looking up at the deer too and then turned back around.

"Me? Don't even own a gun," Stanley said. "How about you, Mr. Fisher? Do you shoot?"

Elwood slid the key off the counter. "I'd think everyone up here would."

"Up here," Grace said, "alone." She turned again and peered out to the dark road, to 395.

Stanley laughed. "Well, when you own a motel you're never alone, not in the way you mean anyway. Nothing to be afraid of."

A gust of wind rattled the window and the door. The bells jangled lightly, and for a moment they all turned toward it as if it were going to open.

"We heard on the radio there might be a storm coming in," Elwood said.

"Snow," Grace said.

"Anything's possible, late spring being so unpredictable up here," Stanley said. "Worse thing is you get stranded for a day or two. Nothing to worry about—I have space."

"Good night," Elwood said, holding the door open as Grace stepped through. Stanley stood there for a moment, watching the door slowly close behind them. He peered at the dangling bells. Next time they jangled, who knew—in would walk Lorna and then it would all be over. To hell with moving on. He walked out from behind the counter, locked the door, then went back around and pulled out the autopsy report.

Inyo County Coroner's Office
Case # 001475-45E-2012
Lorna Uribe
The autopsy is started at 8:00 a.m. The body, encased
in a black body bag and clad in dark gray pajamas and
a light green floral top, is that of a normally developed
white female measuring 63 inches and weighing 125
pounds. No scars or tattoos are present. The body is
cold and unembalmed. Eyes are open. Irises are hazel.
Hair is reddish brown, straight and fine, and measures
12 inches in length. No evidence of medical interven-
tion is present. The body is well preserved and cold due
to refrigeration. Rigor mortis is fully developed.

His neck stiffening, Stanley rubbed it as he scanned downward, his eyes jumping from one subheading to another:

Respiratory System
The left lung weighs 475 grams, and the right lung
weighs 400 grams. Subpleural anthracotic pigment is
found in the lobes. Mucus is…
Gastrointestinal System
The gastric lining of the stomach is unremarkable. No
sign of inflammation is present. The pancreas has…
Cardiovascular System
The heart weighs 270 grams. Postmortem clots are
contained in the great vessels. The circumference of
the aortic valve is…

Stanley flipped to the last page, to the very bottom.

Cause of Death: Undetermined. Lesions of unknown
origin on the heart require further investigation.

And beneath it the only human thing, the looping *H* and *L*, the
signature of Dr. Henri LeBeau, M. D. Stanley slipped the report

back in the envelope. Reaching under the counter, he flipped on the No Vacancy sign and then turned off the light.

Grace sat on the bed. Though its outer edge was firm, she could feel the dip of the valley where the mattress went soft, and she looked around the room, from the chipped nightstands to the dark paneled walls up to the painting above the dresser of a spotted fawn in a meadow, gazing back at her. She'd seen all this before, of course, but it troubled her all the same. "This is such a lonely place," she said.

"You're tired. That's all," Elwood said, pulling shirts out of his suitcase and putting them in a drawer. "It's a long drive."

"I don't see the point of unpacking," she said. "Not for a night. What if the storm comes in?"

"Just wind right now. Like the man said, it's nothing to worry about." Elwood closed his suitcase and headed to the bathroom, a can of shaving cream and a razor in his hands.

Grace got off the bed, went over to the door, and studied the motel map, the escape route in case of emergency, each room a little box with a number on it, an X on theirs. *Should smoke fill the room, get down low and crawl on your stomach. Before opening the door, feel for heat. Do not touch the doorknob.* She'd seen plenty of news footage of high-rise fires, people hanging out windows, smoke billowing, and she'd never forgotten how her best friend's brother, a handsome, strapping football player, had been trampled to death in a fire at a high school dance, only one exit out. Now, at the motel door, Grace peered through the peephole where everything, caught in a bubble, looked miniature, distorted. What if Jared were to suddenly appear in it, back from some forgotten town, having become an outcast Mormon or a Castaneda disciple—Carlos Castaneda that man who wrote books about Indian mystics leading lost young men on vision quests deep in the desert. Jared, lying on the couch one summer, one of those books dangling from his hand, had tried to explain the Castaneda concept of *stopping the world.* "You do it with your eyes, by crossing your eyes," he'd said. Then she hadn't given stopping the world a second thought, not until Jared had disappeared and her world had stopped, and she'd noticed all those books on his shelves and, skimming them, began to wonder.

"Expecting someone?" Elwood asked, coming up behind her.

Grace turned around. "That man—Stanley Uribe," she said, and turned back to the map, even though she was still thinking about Castaneda, an old man now she supposed, living in LA with his disciples, women he called witches who believed the sorcery stuff in his books to be true. She'd read a little about him.

"You know it's only in the movies that the strange guy is the murderer," Elwood said.

"Is it?" Grace said, vacantly, even though she knew Stanley Uribe had been cleared a long time ago, along with everyone else who'd had contact with Jared. But, still, it so bothered her, Stanley Uribe being one of the last to have seen Jared alive, Castaneda being so close to Death Valley, that she couldn't help but become fixated at times. Grace opened the door and stepped outside. Standing beneath the overhang, she shivered as a gust of wind came through, sending the small lantern above her swaying.

2

The next morning after Stanley had cleared away the donuts and muffins from the office, the usual Continental breakfast, he headed down to the Fisher's room, their son's registration card in hand. But no answer at the door, he unlocked it only to find an unmade bed, a few dollars on the pillow, key on the dresser, evidence of a hasty escape. Bypassing check-out was the guest's prerogative, but it irked him, the Fishers cutting out like that, especially since the storm turned out to be a dud, just leaves and branches strewn across the parking lot. The lights hadn't even blown. He looked at the card again, the boy's print—*JARED FISHER*—and then stepped back outside, watching cars go by, and across the street at the white-shingled Bridgeport Bed & Breakfast, a little plume of smoke rising from its chimney, people behind the curtained windows eating hot eggs or pancakes. Still, he had the pool and the Walker River running behind his place.

"Say, what are you doing? Maid quit again?" It was his relief man Cody, a retired railroad worker his father's age in his usual plaid jacket and jeans, a shock of white hair.

"You're on now, aren't you?" Stanley said.

"Why else would I be here? Anything I should know?"

Stanley handed him the room key. "This one needs cleaning. There's something I got to do today." He went back to his office, grabbed his keys, and then went out to his truck. On 395, he headed the same direction as the Fishers, pressing hard on the accelerator, thinking he could catch them, but what would they think, him running up to their car as if they'd forgotten something—a sack of money, underwear, wigs, false teeth, whips, prosthetic limbs, even live animals—what people left behind, the lost and found. Out of the town now and into forest, trees still stirring, a remnant of last night's storm, Stanley glanced over at the card, which was lying on the seat now, and then looked back at the road, the dense trees on either side, half expecting the boy suddenly to slip through, come around the truck and slide in beside him. Then he'd have good reason to rush up behind the Fishers—hero or suspect—and maybe, throwing their grateful arms around him, they'd thank him or maybe Sheriff Boyd would cuff him. But likely the Fishers were hours ahead. He pressed on the accelerator anyway, up ahead Lee Vining, a small settlement near the intersection of 395 and 120, the latter highway the route through Yosemite's high country. Then he started braking, a coyote up ahead. He'd seen his share but never at mid-morning alongside 395. Inching up beside it, Stanley rolled down his window, and the coyote stopped and turned toward him, its topaz eyes blazing, a strip of rabbit or squirrel hanging from its bloody muzzle. Then, turning sharply, it cut into the forest. Rolling up his window, he kept driving, passing through Lee Vining, the usual motel-restaurant strip and a lone school with a fenced-in playground, and on the outskirts The Mono Motel, cabins freshly painted after last summer's wildfire, perched on an embankment above Mono Lake. Then up ahead he saw a familiar turn off and took it, driving along a short, rough patch of road, turning into the Mono Lake Park.

After pulling into a spot, he reached over and slid the boy's card into the glove compartment, then sat there transfixed by the park, with its rolling green lawn tilting down toward the lake, a swing set and picnic tables, where he might have brought his own children had it worked out with Caitlin. Not that they hadn't tried. He put the truck in reverse, but instead of turning back onto 395 to go home, he continued up the rough road. The higher up he went the rougher the road got the more his truck creaked, rolling over broken, weedy pavement. After parking along a chain-link fence, well above the lake now, he got out and pushed open a gate. No flowers, no lawns, no gaudy ornaments, here the dead were clustered in pods, each pod sectioned off by a low wrought-iron fence. Between the pods were graveled walkways that crunched beneath his feet. He liked the sound of it, and maybe the dead did too, the sound of human feet. Her pod was off to the right, close to the main fence where a shallow embankment dropped off into a reedy wetland and then below to the lake's beach. Lorna lay beside another woman with a simple gray footstone, Mary Elizabeth Jones: 1924-1956. Like Lorna, she'd died young, but it was the woman's epitaph— *She lived by the side of the road*—that had always puzzled him, and sometimes he'd splice the two together, her epitaph and Lorna's—*Much too soon*—so it became *she lived by the side of the road much too soon* or *much too soon she lived by the side of the road,* fortune-cookie wordplay he and Lorna would have laughed at.

Stanley walked over to the fence and peered out to the sil-ver-blue lake. The sun was out now, warming the back of his neck, but the chilly wind kept him from loitering. Hands stuffed in his pockets, he headed back to his truck, passing Mary Elizabeth Jones again. A small white house, crab grass, a woman in a plaid dress, alone, lonely—much too soon. What kind of life could be lived by the side of the road? In his truck he turned around and headed back down the road until he saw another car coming up, stopping beside him. He rolled down his window.

"Thought I might find you here," Sheriff Boyd said.

"That's the problem with a small town," Stanley said.

"Listen, coroner has news. Something to show you. Slides of some sort. Pictures he wants you to look at."

Stanley looked down at his hand on the steering wheel, his bandaged finger. "But I haven't even finished—"

"Sometimes things happen fast. And you have to move on it. It's important. The coroner—he said your life and Lorna's boy could be in danger. Don't ask me to explain. I'm not a doctor. Just do what the man asks. Call him." He rolled his window up and started to back out.

Stanley watched the hood of his car disappear down the hill, and then he slowly followed, turning off again into the park, pulling into a spot, suddenly stupefied, thinking how miserable all the waiting had been—the nightmares, the insomnia—and now suddenly an answer. Relieved, elated is what he should have felt, but sitting in his truck, peering out at the grassy park,

two swings swaying slightly in the wind, he felt oddly disorient-
ed, deflated. He thought of his mother, her eyes rolling into the
back of her head, the doctor's description of her hospital death
meant to ease him, but now when he thought of her he couldn't
rid himself of that image. So maybe Sheriff Boyd had been
right about information not being such a good thing.

He got out of his truck and cut across the grass, past the
picnic tables and swings, to the boardwalk that sliced through
a thicket of reeds, cover for small birds. There, walled in and
out of sight, he slowed down, the planks creaking beneath his
weight as he inhaled, the pungent smell of sage and pickleweed
calming him. Once out of the reeds, he saw the lake spread
before him, the silvery-blue flatness, the curls of white caps,
and out in the distance the brilliant white tufa rising up, carved
by water into various human shapes, and all the hundreds of
waterfowl resting on the lake. At the end of the boardwalk was
a small lookout with a wooden bench and beside it the Maid
of the Lake, what everyone called her, the lake's resident bird
expert, the old bird stationed at her post with all the other birds.

"Hey, Myra."

She turned around, stiff and sudden. "Jesus, you gave me
a start, spying on me like that, Stanley Uribe. Could have killed
me, snuck up behind me and throttled my shriveled-up turkey
neck."

Stanley laughed. "No offense, Myra, but you're not particularly killable, even with your turkey neck."

"Haven't seen you for a long time. How's business?" Binoculars hanging from her neck, she wore the beige park uniform
and a tall, brimmed hat that dwarfed her. Beneath it, her sunken
blue eyes beamed like marbles.

"Better than yours. Where's everybody?"

She glanced at her watch. "Breakfast. Tourists got to eat.
Sometimes food beats out a lake full of fowl. We won't be alone
for long though."

Stanley looked back at the boardwalk and then down at the
bench where Myra's dog-eared book *Mono Lake Birds* sat and

beside it the spare pair of binoculars she always kept around for tourists. He reached for the binoculars and scanned the lake.

"You visiting Lorna?" she asked. "They ever find out what happened? People been wondering."

Stanley lowered the binoculars.

"How many months has it been?" she asked.

"Some people never find out. They just die and no one knows why" slipped out of Stanley's mouth—something Caitlin had told him years ago when they'd been together. Lying on the couch in her scrubs, she'd played dead, eyes open, staring at nothing, and then blinked and laughed, punchy after a double hospital shift.

"Oh baloney. Only old women like me die in their sleep. Or poor little babies." Myra lifted her binoculars, training them on the lake. "It's a raucous group this year. All that racket out there. It's a wonder they keep away from each other—the gulls over there, the geese over here, the phalaropes over there. You know those little birds fly over 3000 miles to the Andes without stopping. Head out again in September, always sneaking away in the middle of the night. No one knows why." She put her binoculars down and looked over at Stanley. "How about poison? I hear it's hard to detect."

"Who'd want to do that?"

Myra shrugged. "Someone with something to gain. Her ex maybe."

"He's got an alibi, lives in another state."

"Well, then, how about you?"

"Me?" Stanley chuckled.

"Not knowing. Well, you can't leave things like that. As bad as that boy who disappeared awhile back in the desert. What was his name?"

"Jared Fisher. His parents were just here again as a matter of fact, stayed in the motel last night, same room as their son. Three years in a row."

"No kidding."

"They cut out in the middle of the night though, the parents." Stanley nodded toward the lake. "Just like your little birds." He laid the binoculars back on the bench.

"Something spook them?" Myra asked.

"The wind? Themselves. Ghosts. Me? Who knows?"

"They still think you had something to do with it?"

"I think they think anyone and everyone who saw their son up here had something to do with it."

"I guess that's less painful than thinking *you* had something to do with it, your own kid running away or killing himself if that's what happened. But what about your sister?"

Stanley hesitated. He picked up the binoculars again and trained them on the boardwalk, expecting Sheriff Boyd to be loping down it, scowling, wondering why he was dawdling, wasn't hightailing it back, on the phone to the coroner.

"Stanley?"

"The coroner. He wants to speak to me."

"So there is news."

"Just found out."

"That's good. It means they know something."

Stanley put the binoculars down again and looked over at Myra.

"Oh." She nodded. "So now you don't want to know. The truth got you scared, huh?"

Grace felt bad. Earlier she'd rushed Elwood out of bed and past Mono Lake and the tufa he'd wanted to take pictures of. All night in Bridgeport while Elwood had slept she'd been up and down, peeking between the curtains as the wind howled, scattering debris across the parking lot. Before dawn, worried they'd get stranded, she'd shaken Elwood awake, but even after they'd packed and rushed out she could see there really was no threat. No sleet. No snow. No downed power lines. Still, as they'd turned on to 395, the road so dark and empty it normally would have scared her, she'd felt relieved as if she'd escaped something, not fire but something more sinister. Maybe it was the long drive, as Elwood had suggested, arriving at night, passing through the strip of dreary motels and dimly lit gas stations surrounded by dark forest, or the motel itself, the room, though backing the river, as dark and dreary as the rest of the town, that had depressed her, even though she knew, kept telling herself that nothing bad had happened there, Jared and his friends leaving the next morning, as she and Elwood had this morning, driving into Death Valley. But now some 2000 feet lower, well beneath Mono Lake, all she could say was "maybe we can stop on the way back," as they continued dropping into the arid bowl of the Owens Valley, 395 running between the dry Inyo mountains and the snow-laced Sierras, the city of Bishop sprawling below them.

"Or next year, on the way up," Elwood said. "We never drive back this way. Takes too long. It's I-5 most of the way back. Remember?"

"That's right," she said. "I hate that route." The flat valley, the feedlots, the cows perched on manure mounds. The smell. It made her understand why women went to nunneries, men to monasteries, why people ran away. At first, though, she couldn't understand why Jared wanted to go to Death Valley for spring break, her first impression of it, barren and featureless, endless spans of sand and rock, a few scrawny wildflowers clinging to the road's edge. But last spring, after she'd settled into an uneasy existence, a truce of sorts, Jared's silent bedroom looming down the hallway, she began to feel differently, to better understand. Maybe that's why she'd dragged Elwood out of the motel so early, rushing him past the lake.

On the outskirts of Bishop now, Elwood pulled into a gas station. Cars. Trucks. Campers. The pumps nearly full, people were streaming in and out of the store, others cleaning windshields, scraping off debris and dead moths. Grace got out and stretched, peering next door over at *The Paiute Royal Casino*, its neon sign rising like a giant lollipop, flashing *Open 24 Hours*, cars parked every which way as if disaster had suddenly struck and everyone had pulled off hastily fleeing inside. Across the street cows grazed. Nothing had changed. While Elwood pumped

gas, Grace walked over to the store, its sliding glass door opening and closing as people passed in and out, a mishmash of
flyers taped to it: *Paiute Tribal Counsel to Hear the Case of Sam
Waters April 23, 4:00 p.m. Missing Hiker Last Seen on Lawson Trail
near Groveland. May Be Sick. Chicken Plucker Needed. Pay in Chick-
ens. (760) 825-5662. Tired? Depressed? Weekly Support Meetings.
Bishop First Congregational Church.* She walked back to the car and
looked over at the casino again. "No one's gone in or out since
we've been here. And all those cars—isn't that strange?"

Elwood laughed. "We haven't been here that long." He
pulled out the nozzle, screwed the gas cap back on. "Ready?"
On 395 again they passed more ranchland and a hodgepodge
of small antique shops and Mexican cantinas. "Amazing, isn't
it?" he said.

Grace assumed he meant the contrast, the ramshackle town
set up against the majestic mountains. That's how a lot of the
Sierra Nevada was, spectacular scenery, dumpy towns.

"The temperature change," Elwood said. "So cold in Bridgeport and not a cloud in the sky here and warm. You know that
photographer—did I tell you about him? The one that just died
in the airplane crash—he has a gallery in town."

Grace looked back at the casino, its sign still visible. "There's
an Indian reservation around here somewhere. Or maybe we're
already in it."

"There's one in Death Valley too, isn't there?" Elwood said.

"The Timbisha Shoshone. The woman who checks us in at
the Ranch lives on it. She told me pack rides go right through
their land where the radio station is, the one her husband runs.
Remember how he made an announcement about Jared?"
Grace gazed blankly out the window. "But there aren't many
Indians left there. She said it's hard making a living there. They
have to sell snow cones and Navajo tacos."

Elwood slowed down, the traffic becoming heavier as they
entered downtown Bishop and motel row, blue pools and more
neon signs mixed in with fast food, banks, a movie theater.
Elwood stopped at a light. On one side of the street was a Mc-

Donald's, yellow arches and busy drive-through, on the other side Bishop First Congregational, on its front lawn a marquee.

"What's it say this time?" Elwood asked. "Last year's was pretty clever."

"*Served over 2 billion.* Shouldn't it say *saved* over 2 billion?"

"Then it wouldn't be half as funny," Elwood said, the light turning green.

Grace pulled out a map and started unfolding it. "How far's the turn off for Panamint Springs?"

"We still have a ways. There's Big Pine, then Independence. We can stop there to eat if you want."

"Or up at Panamint Springs."

"Food's pretty bad there and expensive," Elwood said.

"It's pretty bad everywhere up here."

"I like Independence, the county seat," Elwood said. "Less congested than Bishop. Big trees. Nice shade. Pretty court-house. Wide streets then suddenly the mountains. Nothing in between."

Grace started folding the map back up.

"Galen Rowell," Elwood said. "That's his name, the photographer, the one that died. Look, it's right over there, his gallery, on the corner, the white brick building with the green awnings. His wife died too."

"That's a shame," Grace said as they passed it. "Looks closed."

The town started thinning out. After they passed a California Highway Patrol building, they were surrounded by ranchland again, tall grasses and cattle and eventually came to Big Pine. Population 845. "Can that many people live here?" Grace said, as a squat motel, another gas station, a general store, and then more open land passed. When they reached Independence, its two-block downtown, the tall, shuttered windows of a Victorian hotel came into view, and across from it the grand court-house, its gold-framed doors sparkling, a sprawling oak shading its deep lawn where three years ago she and Elwood had stood stiffly beside an Inyo County sheriff on the courthouse steps asking the public for help. Then later, back in their Death Valley motel room, they'd watched themselves, their own faces on the news, Elwood's contorted, hers stony.

"Next is Lone Pine," Elwood said. "The Alabama Hills where they filmed all the old westerns and then the ranger station."

"Each town gets smaller, doesn't it? Soon it'll just be the two of us," Grace said.

"Somewhere around here is Whitney Portal, up higher, on the Sierra side. Acclimate overnight then hike up the next morning."

"I think we're too old for that," Grace said.

"People older than us climb it."

"And people younger than us die on it."

"Okay," Elwood said. "Here we go." Slowing down, he turned, pulling into a ranger station and then into a spot between a car and a van. "Pretty crowded here. Last pit stop before Panamint Springs."

"You go. I'll wait here," Grace said.

"You sure? It's a long ways before another flush toilet."

"I'm fine. Really." Grace watched Elwood walk up the sidewalk and head toward the restrooms; then she got out. Standing alongside the van, its door open, she could see stacked cages inside, in them dogs panting, yelping.

"Afternoon," she heard someone call out, and she turned and saw a man with a red bandana around his neck coming down the sidewalk toward her. Breathing heavily, he was carrying two water jugs and wearing a red T-shirt—*Death Valley Live or Die*, a hiking skeleton beneath—stained at the armpits. He nodded at her, then hopped up inside the van, and started filling bowls and sliding them in the cages.

"Where are you taking them?" Grace asked.

Crouched down on his heels, the man swiveled toward her. "Inyo County Shelter. For adoption. The lucky ones anyway. The rest of them, well… You have pets?"

"A cat. Duke. My son's."

"No dogs?" The man hopped out of the van.

Grace shook her head. "I wouldn't think there'd be that many strays out here."

"There's strays everywhere."

"How long have you been a dogcatcher?"

"Long enough."

"And you like it?"

"Now that's a funny question." Smirking, he cocked his head to the side and rubbed his chin. "I guess you could say I do." He looked back into the van at the dogs and then turned back to her. "Say, why don't you have a look? Quick before your hubby gets back. I can see you're an animal lover. Come on. Hop up." He put out his hand.

Grace looked down at it, at the scratches on it.

He pulled his hand back and shrugged. "Okay, so they don't all go easy."

Grace stepped closer, peering inside at a small, yapping dog, long-haired and reddish with floppy ears.

"See. She likes you. That's Ginger. Well, I don't know her real name—I just made it up. Come on now. Duke won't mind. Duke and Ginger. I'll even throw in some food."

"We're on our way to Death Valley."

"No problem. Pick one out now and you can swing by the shelter on the way back and pick him up."

"Actually we take a different route back."

"How come?"

"It's what we do every year."

The man pulled the bandana off his neck and wiped his forehead. "What's your name?"

"Grace."

"Grace. Now I won't pretend to understand, but here you can save a life. It's in your hands."

Grace looked around the parking lot, at people getting in and out of cars, filing in and out of the restrooms. They were hardly alone. She squinted in the bright sunlight. "Have you asked any of them?"

"*Them* is the reason we're here right now. *Them* is why I exist, but you're different. Could tell right away. There's a reason for everything. So what do you say? Why not take two? The larger ones are in the back."

Grace glanced back again at the restrooms, wondering what had happened to Elwood.

"Now come on, Grace. No time to procrastinate when a life's at stake, right? What a woman thinks of herself determines her fate. You're a smart person. I know you know what that means. Now, come on." He held his hand out again.

Grace looked down at it, the scratches and the deep lines, swooping and broken. "I'm sorry. I can't," she said, backing away.

"Okay, Grace," he said, dropping his hand, whistling a little between his teeth. "It was a pleasure…" He hopped back in the van, and the dogs, rushing forward, started barking. Then the door slid shut.

"Who's that?" Elwood said, coming up behind Grace.

She watched the van back out.

"Grace?"

"The dogcatcher of Inyo County."

"Out here?"

"Where were you?"

"I stopped in the ranger station to buy a few postcards. What's wrong? You look upset."

"He wanted me to adopt a dog."

Elwood glanced in the backseat. "You didn't, did you?"

"He said they all get put down, the ones that don't get adopted."

"Well, this isn't the Bay Area."

"I know. But…" Grace looked over at him and then got in the car.

"What?" Elwood said, getting in the driver's seat.

"You must be tired," she said, though she knew he liked driving. Driving, he'd always said, took his mind off things and put his mind on other things. "Your eyes are bloodshot."

"I just got a new prescription." He tapped the edge of his glasses and then started the car and backed out.

Grace crossed her legs and watched the road ahead pitch up

toward the sky. Resting her elbow on the door, she waited for the first rise and dip and curve of the road, but she couldn't get the dogs out of her mind, their anxious eyes. The last time she'd brought Duke in for his checkup, she'd had a long wait, the apologetic vet explaining how a dog he was trying to put down wouldn't die. It had never occurred to her that it could take so long. Grace grabbed onto the door handle as the car took a curve.

"It's like a little roller coaster," Elwood said, "isn't it?" They arced around another corner, through a short, narrow canyon. Small yellow daises and green shrubbery sprouted from the dark rocky walls. Out her window she could see a drop-off, then a dry expanse of barren valley, and beyond that a series of low-lying ridges and fissures snaking through another distant canyon. A woman from the grief therapy group she and Elwood had been attending, who'd visited Death Valley, had left early, claiming there was nothing to see, but Grace knew there was a lot to see or a lot that couldn't be seen. You had to look hard.

Elwood gave Grace a sidelong glance. "I can practically hear you thinking."

Grace laughed. "You must be Superman then."

"I am," he said. "With my new glasses. With my superhuman sight I can see into people's minds."

She tapped her temple. "So, what am I thinking?"

"You're thinking… Well, you have to be willing. Otherwise, it doesn't work, right?"

"I see," she said.

"So, what are you thinking?" he asked.

"Nothing."

"So, you're a Buddhist now?"

"Hardly. Psychics. That's what I'm thinking. You know that woman from the group, the doctor's wife—their daughter gassed herself in the garage—went to a psychic. To see if her daughter was happy, you know, in heaven, if she blamed them."

"Or hell—if she's a Catholic."

"Actually, it was a channeler, someone who speaks for the

dead, and this channeler told her it *was* her fault, the suicide."

"No kidding," Elwood said. "So much for psychics telling people what they want to hear."

"Or maybe that was what she wanted to hear. You know, to put an end to it. To know at least. Even if it is your fault."

"Or not. So, what did you say?"

"What can you say?"

"You're not thinking of going to a channeler, are you?"

"Me?"

"Then why were you thinking about it?"

"I don't know." She sighed. "That man. With the dogs. His hands. They were all scratched up."

"The dogcatcher? He was just messing with you, Grace," Elwood said, one hand resting on the bottom of the steering wheel, the other dangling out the window, now that they'd come out of the curves and were on a straightaway.

Grace flipped down the visor, glancing at her face, then flipped it back up. "I don't want to go back to the grief therapy group anymore."

"What? Because of the dogcatcher? What did he say to you?"

"I don't see the point. It doesn't make me feel any better. It's morbid. All those people with their dead or missing children."

"But, Grace, we are those people. Besides, I like talking to people. Most people do."

"Then why not go bowling?"

"That's ridiculous. It's just that you don't like anyone. You never have. No wonder that man picked on you."

"What's that supposed to mean?"

"You think you can figure things out yourself."

Grace sighed and shook her head. "It's not a criticism. I don't blame them, of course. It's just how I feel."

"What exactly did that man say to you?"

"It's nothing to do with him, Elwood," she said, even though she couldn't help glance out her window at the outer mirror, unable to shed the feeling that one hill back, just out of sight, someone was following. *We cast a shadow on something wherever we stand, and it is no good moving from place to place to save things;*

because the shadow always follows, something she'd found scribbled on a scrap of paper, along with other scribblings, in Jared's desk drawer.

Elwood glanced up in his rearview mirror. "What are you looking at?"

"Just the Joshua trees. How they just start up out of nowhere."

"They look like people, don't they?" Elwood said, "but kind of twisted."

"The Mormons named them after the prophet, the trees being their only welcome."

Elwood nodded. "Well, it must have been lonely being the first one."

Having left Mono Lake, Stanley was back in Bridgeport driving toward his motel, the voices of Sheriff Boyd and Myra swirling in his head. *You could be in danger. Do what the man asks. Scared, huh?* Then he saw his own sign—The Sleepy River Lodge—in the rearview mirror start shrinking away, and he tried to ease up, to slow himself down as he sped through the rest of town, thinking that maybe all the misery, the not knowing had somehow fueled him, cocooned him, and now without it he didn't know what to do. In ranchland now, he felt a little better, less anxious as he passed a few small houses set deep, mountains looming behind them, and cows at the road's fence line, heads between the slats, chewing lazily. Born, eat, be eaten. Maybe the cows had it better. He switched on his signal, ahead the turn-off for Route 108 to the Sonora Pass, a route he'd driven many times. Normally still snowed in this time of year, the road had opened early due to last winter's light snowfall. Climbing steeply via switchbacks, the narrow road took him quickly up into an even darker forest of pines, sequoias, and the tall, lean aspen that clung to the roadside. Pretty as it was, he tried to keep his eyes on the yellow line dividing the road, wary of the steep drop off. Let go of the wheel, and over the edge he'd tumble never to be found, but then his father, bedridden in a nursing home, in its Memory Wing, would be on his own. True, his father still sometimes remembered him, but each visit it seemed harder, and if Sheriff Boyd were right, that he really was in danger, that he might beat his father to the grave, what then was the point of living? His front-desk man Cody, shaking his head, had waved questions like that away, both his parents having lived into triple digits. "Damn good genes, Lipton tea, lots of walking, and love," he'd said. That was the problem with longevity—you couldn't argue with it. Still, Stanley, shifting his eyes from the yellow line, couldn't help but look over the edge until the sound of a horn, not loud, just a *tap, tap, tap* brought him back—a couple on the other side in a shiny red hatchback, craning their faces toward him, waving. A golden retriever, its head out the window, fur flying, barked. Following custom, he raised his hand too and in his rearview mirror watched the happy car disappear. Then he rolled up his window, the air getting cooler, the trees thinning out as he approached the pass, a cold, barren place with few turn-offs and a trail or two; the last one he'd hiked with Caitlin, up a long-extinct volcano, brilliant wild flowers springing up from black shale, then a freak hail storm driving them under an overhang that opened at the other end to a drop-off, where Caitlin had told him she was pregnant.

At 9,400 feet now, at the pass, Stanley turned off, pulling into a small parking lot, a light-green National Forest pickup there, a horse trailer attached to it. Several feet away was an outhouse. He put on his jacket and walked over to a picnic table and sat down, taking in the view, the humps of sun-lit mountains pushing against each other, granite glittering between patches of trees. It was cold up here though, and he shivered, wishing he'd brought a warmer jacket. He smelled smoke and heard a snort and saw in the distance a horse lassoed between two trees, a small one-man tent and a ranger kneeling at a fire pit, rising to his feet. Walking toward Stanley, he tipped his hat. "Didn't think I'd see anyone up here all day."

"Kind of cold to be camping. The wind must have been bad here last night," Stanley said.

"Mountain lion census."

"That's why you're here? How many so far?"

"Not a one."

"Then how do you know they're here?"

"The hunting ban and plenty of deer. Plus, the females they scream. Every night. And my horse goes crazy."

Stanley looked over at the animal, sniffing the ground, tail twitching. "Can't say I blame it. You aren't worried? Up here by yourself."

The ranger chuckled and nodded toward Stanley's truck. "You're far more likely to be killed in your vehicle than by a lion."

"Sure, if you're not the one being killed, like that woman down in Sonora. The runner a few years back."

"We shot that cat—a mother trying to feed her kittens. So, what brings you up here? Kind of late for hiking."

"Heading down to Sonora."

"That where you're from?"

"Not anymore. You?"

"Stationed in Strawberry but grew up in Berkeley."

"You know The Fielding Hotel there? The motel I run I bought from a guy whose father owned it. A swanky place apparently."

"Sure. Nearly burned down a few years ago. Fire came right up to the back of it."

Stanley stood up and pulled out his keys. "Well, stay safe."

"You as well." The ranger lifted his hand and then turned toward his camp.

Stanley started up his truck, letting it idle as he watched the ranger stoking up his fire, the smoke swirling up into the air. Then he got back onto 108, passing through Strawberry, Mi-Wuk, and Twain Harte, a larger, more developed town with a new shopping center and houses, old A-Frames mixed in with newer construction; then, he was dropping down into the foothills, closing in on Sonora, population 4223, the sign said. Slowing down, he turned off, passing through the downtown— wooden boardwalks and antique shops, once Gold Rush saloons—where he and Lorna had hung out as kids when they weren't running around in the woods hoping to get hopelessly lost until dinner time. Warmer down here, he rolled down the windows and drove a short steep hill up to a bluff, pulled into the lot, and parked. Sitting there, he peered at the old three-story brick building, a former insane asylum turned nursing home, with expansive, grassy grounds and blooming flowers, wrought-iron benches. Hardly anyone ever sat out there though, except for today, an aide in pink scrubs, legs crossed, smoking. That's how these places were—he and Lorna had looked at several— nice outside, not so nice inside. An old motel trick: great lobby, dumpy rooms. Curb appeal. Though that wasn't the case for his motel. Dumpy lobby, dumpy rooms. Honest at least. He looked over at the entrance, above it a snazzy red scalloped awning you might find at a fancy restaurant, *The Sonora* written on it in white cursive. Opening his door, he swung one leg out and then stopped. He looked over at the passenger seat, on the floor an old newspaper, a title catching his attention.

WOMAN KILLS SON IN MENDOCINO COUNTY NURSING HOME

Yesterday two people were found dead in an apparent murder-suicide in the Lands End Nursing Home in Laverty, a small coastal town in Northern California. Laverty Police Chief Delmore Watkins said nursing home staff found Eleanor Swift, 56, and her son Dylan, 25, dead from single gunshot wounds to the head. Mrs. Swift's son was paralyzed as a result of a motorcycle accident five years ago. Unhappy with her son's care, Mrs. Swift moved her son from one facility to another. Her son, who claimed his caretakers taunted him, calling him "fat," "useless," and "better off dead," said he wanted to die. A note Mrs. Swift sent to KPF News Anchor Kyle Reed indicated she could no longer bear to see her son suffer.

He'd never seen anything like that in his father's facility. He'd met all his father's aides, but then who knew what went on

when no one was looking. Lorna had fretted over putting their
father in a facility, but neither of them could care for him once
he became bedridden, and, after they'd put him in, she'd fretted over visiting him, afraid anything she came in contact with
might contaminate her, give her some disease. That was what
he'd withheld from Sheriff Boyd—her obsession with disease
and germs, her fear something was coming to get her, a dark
shadow trailing one step behind her. So it was always on him
to visit.

He got out of the car, walked across the lot, and headed
down the steps to the scalloped awning, the entrance below
ground where no bellman greeted him. Though he wasn't
religious, despite his mother's insistence on childhood church
attendance, he began to think that hell, if it existed, resided in
the diffused purple-gray light of buzzing fluorescent rods that
never burned hot enough to burn out and faded floral wallpaper where, because the seams didn't line up, certain flowers
were truncated, missing half their petals or simply mismatched,
strange floating mutations. In the lobby he'd only noticed this
because his father had been such a perfectionist about wallpa-
pering, lining up foil petals or butterfly wings for his mother
on their bathroom walls. He signed in at the reception desk
and then headed toward the elevators. Though his father was
on the third floor, he preferred to take the steps, but they were
alarmed. A code had to be punched in. He knew the code, but
it still made him uneasy—he might set the alarm off, someone thinking he was an escapee—so he rode the elevator up.
Large and rectangular, it needed to accommodate stretchers,
and alone in it he felt as if he were standing in a large white
cavernous room as it lifted him up with a groan and let him
off, its doors slowly parting. Then, once in the hallway, it wasn't
long before an odor wafted into his nostrils. Disinfectant, shit,
cooked food, all of it morphing into the odor of decay—this
was how he'd deconstructed it. Now to get to the Memory
Wing, or *the dark side* as he'd overheard an aide once call it, he
had to pass through a set of locked doors. Painted on them was
a mural, a bucolic scene, a path leading through a bright green

grassy field of trees, birds chirping on branches, the words *This Way* painted at the top, leading the way. He pressed a red button on the wall, and the charge nurse buzzed him in.

"Good afternoon, Mr. Uribe. Nice to see you again. Your father's awake."

He started down the hallway, passing residents slumped in wheelchairs or standing against the wall quietly staring or glaring at him. A wheelchair-bound woman parked near the nurse's station, asleep in front of a TV, was clutching a Raggedy Ann doll, while a drooling man his age—the young brain-damaged ones ended up here too—in an electric wheelchair, buzzed down the hallway, a can of Pepsi teetering on his tray. Stanley looked back down the hallway to the doors from which he had entered, the same mural painted on the inside, the same words *This Way* leading out. But Stanley had gotten used to this, the way in and out; the man in room 306, the room right before his father's, was another matter though. *Just because the door's open doesn't mean you have to look,* his mother would have admonished him as a child, taking him by the hand at the local carnival, rushing him past the sideshow freaks. But now there was no hand pulling him away and so, as he had each time he'd visited, he took a quick peek. The man, well over six feet, emaciated, draped in a white sheet, was stretched out on an inclined dental chair in his usual position, head turned toward him, mouth gaping open, his steel-blue eyes, fixed and dazzling, looking right at him. A woman was in there too—he'd seen her before—the daughter, he assumed, on a stool, spoon in one hand, a baby-food jar in the other. But now he was at his father's room where another man, this one short and stout, sat perched on the edge of the bed in striped pajamas, feet dangling, a model airplane in his hands.

"Hello, Nathan," Stanley said.

The man raised his eyes to Stanley's. "On a mission tonight."

"Mum's the word." Stanley passed around the curtain between the beds. "Hey, Dad," he said loudly over his father's TV and then picked up the remote, turning the TV off.

"Hey, why'd you do that for? Who are you?"

"It's me, your son, Stanley." He went over to the wall of

relatives, pictures he'd taped up of his mother and Lorna and his uncle Fermin, his father's brother, as a reminder. "See, this is your family. Your wife. Your daughter. That's your brother." It was the wall of the dead, but at least it might jog his memory, Stanley thought. "And this is me, your son."

"You. I can see you. I'm not an idiot. Do you know where my son is?"

"Right here. In front of you, Dad."

"No, no, no." He wagged his finger. "No tricks on me. It's not Halloween." He laughed, and Stanley laughed with him, and sometimes he wondered if he was faking it.

"So how are you feeling today, Dad? Have you eaten?"

"They don't feed you here."

"There's a tray right there. Right in front of you. Looks like you ate all right." A pint of milk, spout open, chicken bones, string beans, and an unopened applesauce sat on the tray. "You want to get outside, get in the wheelchair today?"

His father cocked his head to the side. "He's a POW."

"Who? Nathan? Isn't he on a mission?"

"Thinks the food's poisoned."

"So you want to get outside before it's too late?"

"I'm waiting for my son. My son always takes me out."

Stanley pointed to Lorna's picture again. It was one of the few grade-school pictures left of her, a sweet one, smiling, despite a missing tooth, in a short-sleeve navy dress, two green stripes of ribbon across the chest. He didn't even have a recent picture, she so hated being photographed. "Dad, do you know who she is?"

"Her? Why's she on my wall? Who are you anyway? A thief? Trying to steal my family, my TV? Is that why you're here?"

"That's Lorna, your daughter. Remember how we all used to go to the lake, Mono Lake? When we were kids. On vacation."

"Kings and queens."

"Yes, the tufa, that's right, Dad. That's what you used to call them. Like chess pieces."

"But," his father shook his head, looking at the wall, "I don't know that girl. How'd she get there?"

❧

After a late lunch at Panamint Springs, Grace and Elwood headed down into the low desert, getting closer to the Furnace Creek Ranch, Grace looking through her window up at the Panamint Mountains. "They're doing digs up there now. At the Manson place. It was in the newspaper."

"As in Charles Manson? Is he still alive?"

"One of those women is up for parole. Wants compassionate release. Breast cancer. She claims there's more victims."

"I didn't even know Manson was in Death Valley. They find anything?"

"Just animal bones." Grace pressed her palm lightly to her abdomen.

Elwood glanced over at her. "What? Car sick?"

She waved her hand. "It's fine."

"I'll slow down."

Grace could feel the car pulling back. She didn't know how to explain it, the fluctuation of emotions the descent into Death Valley brought her. It wasn't just the serpentine road or the lift and drop of the hills but the air itself and the dread and wonder she felt entering the outskirts of the park, in the sand and mountains and brilliant blue sky, the tight canyons or open stretches. Though spring weather was usually temperate, not hot enough to kill, a park ranger had told her how Europeans, fascinated with heat, came in busloads in summer. Heat, though, hadn't been a factor in Jared's disappearance, his car found mid desert, at 2000 feet, not here in the Panamints but in the western part of the park, in the back country, at the Racetrack Playa, a dried-up lakebed between the Cottonwood and Last Chance Mountains, a mystery spot where rocks somehow moved across the playa of their own volition.

"I'm not seeing many wildflowers," Elwood said. "Must have been a dry winter here." He looked over at Grace and then back at the road.

"Just little yellow daises along the road," Grace said.

"I've got plenty of California Gold. Gravel Ghost and Des-

ert Five Spot—that's what I'd like to photograph. Maybe up at
the Ubehebe Crater."

"I wouldn't get your hopes up." Though no expert in wildflowers, Grace thought she could predict what wildflower life
might be like deeper in the park by how plentiful the flowers
were up here in the Panamints on the roadside where they
seemed to grow best. Plus, the crater on a typical day was windy,
whipping itself up into terrible tempests, so bad last year they
couldn't even get their car doors open and had to turn back and
drive out again the next day when it was calmer.

"So what was Manson doing up in the Panamints?" Elwood
asked.

"Holed up in some abandoned ranch, up one of those wash-
es, but the road there is treacherous, yet Manson somehow got
a school bus up. No one knows how."

"And he's still alive?"

"Remember the state got rid of the death penalty, so they all
got life. He's in Corcoran now."

"It's strange to think…who was that actress?"

"Sharon Tate. He's segregated so inmates don't kill him. The
state's full of murderers, you know."

"I guess every state is. Here comes Stovepipe Wells." Elwood slowed down as the motel there appeared in the distance,
a cluster of dark green one-story buildings on one side of the
street, each with a name—Roadrunner, Tamarisk, Buttonwil-
low—pushing back into the desert. Across the street people
sitting on benches ate ice cream in front of the general store.
Besides this motel, the Furnace Creek Ranch and the Furnace
Creek Inn were the only other places to stay in the park.

"I don't need to stop unless you need to," Grace said.

"The Ranch it is then," Elwood said, as they passed Mesquite
Flat, its parking lot full, people way out on the dunes trudging
up steep ridges. Out there summer ground temperatures could
exceed 100 degrees, the few mesquite bushes between the
dunes offering meager shade. Every year the park newspaper
printed the same warning story about someone out too far with
too little water, dying. Next came Devil's Cornfield, a parched,

rocky plane, rows of low-growing, scrappy brush, and then the turn-off for Salt Creek, a spot Jared and his roommates had been to the day before he'd disappeared.

> *Great Place. Hot though. Lots of pup fish. Went off trail. More water, reeds. A lone duck. Horse flies. Ouch! Ran back.*

Jared's postcard had been in their mailbox when they'd returned home from their first fruitless search of the park.

"So what if we stopped there?" Elwood said.

"Where?" Grace looked over her shoulder. "You just passed Salt Creek."

"Corcoran."

Grace laughed.

"I don't suppose Manson gets many visitors."

"What makes you think he'd want to see you? He's got plenty of pen pals, women who want to marry him. He was a career criminal long before anyone heard of him, a con artist. I picked up a book about him last year at the visitor center. I brought it with me if you're interested."

"Okay. Here we are," Elwood said, as the road dropped lower, curving around, and they passed Mustard Canyon, another tourist spot, the remains of an old mining site perched up on a hill, and then the familiar trio of skinny palms towering skyward, their crazy heads blowing in the wind, planted in a triangle of lush green grass, the wooden sign FURNACE CREEK RANCH staked into it. Elwood turned into the parking lot. "I was only kidding about Manson."

"You know they cut her baby out—Sharon Tate. I'll get the keys." Grace opened the door and stepped out into the hot dry air. It felt good, welcoming, unlike the fog of the north, where they lived, sometimes hanging on through whole summer days. As she climbed the four steps up to the check-in building, she looked over at the post office, a cheerful yellow bungalow, the blue mailbox in front where Jared must have dropped his postcard, and beyond that the date grove, date trees tall as palms, moving in the wind. Inside now Grace stepped up to the counter.

"Welcome back, Mrs. Fisher," the woman said.

Grace recognized her right away too, the warm full face, the black hair parted down the center, the whites of her eyes bright, her glasses dangling around her neck on a gold chain, the woman from the Timbisha Shoshone reservation who always helped them. Grace opened her bag and pulled out her wallet.

"Oh, that's not necessary, Mrs. Fisher. We have all your information. We know who you are. Here we go." She pulled two keys from beneath the counter and slid them into a small envelope, on top of which she wrote 842 in black marker. "I'd give you a map, but I think you know your way. Say, have you heard any more about your son? You heard what's going on up in the Panamints, the digs, right?"

"I doubt they're going to find anything up there, and, no, no news about my son, but thank you." Grace took the key and walked out. She opened the car door. "842," she said, getting in.

"I wonder how long they'll keep doing it," Elwood said, as they drove past restaurant row, then the Death Valley Museum, its rusty wagons displayed in front. Pulled by mule teams, the massive wagons transported borax, a mineral used in detergents, to the nearest railway station. In the lot, Elwood parked beneath a tamarisk tree. The motel consisted of four two-story barrack-like buildings, each one numbered 600 through 900, with strips of grassy areas between them; theirs was the 800 building.

After they carried their luggage up to the second floor, Elwood started unpacking while Grace, opening the sliding door, stepped out onto the balcony where another tamarisk, an enormous one, partly blocked her view of the golf course, the lowest in the world. Not that she cared. Pretty as the course was, it was the tamarisk that fascinated her, its thick, muscular branches covered in brittle bark sprouting a veil of feathery green foliage. Sometimes when she couldn't sleep she'd go out there listening to it creak in the night breeze.

Elwood stepped beside her. "Any golfers?"

Grace shifted her gaze from the tree to the greens, two crows hopping around. One, craning its neck toward them, suddenly took flight, landing on the grass closer to them. Shiny black and ungainly, it bounced around, looking up at them, cawing.

Elwood leaned over and called down to it. "Hungry, are you?"

Grace laughed. "Careful what you say. They might remember it."

"I wonder what they eat in the wild."

"Other birds. They're carnivorous. They're like people—they remember faces. The Indians believe it too."

"I didn't know you were such an expert on crows—or Indians."

"It's only mean people that have to worry, the ones that hurt them. See that one? He's still looking at you."

"Well, at least I'll be remembered," Elwood said, and then stepped back into the room. "Time for a shower."

Grace stepped back in too. Two double beds, pastel desert sketches above each, an oak dresser with a TV on top, above that a mirror, and in the corner a small oak table with two upholstered chairs—same as last year, yet still she couldn't help thinking if she only looked hard enough something would reveal itself, like those puzzles, ordinary scenes where only one thing's off and you have to spot it.

After Elwood dressed, they went to dinner at the 49er Café, where they usually ate, and then later, back at the room, Elwood, a magazine open on his chest, promptly fell asleep, snoring lightly. In bed beside him, Grace gently lifted the magazine, skimming a few paragraphs, a Colonel Fawcett disappearing in the Amazon looking for the elusive El Dorado. Then, she shut off the lights and turned the TV down low. Flipping channels, she paused at a jungle scene, a mangrove swamp, a documentary just coming on—*The Zombies of Haiti*. Could the dead or near dead be brought back to life? If the witch doctor got his potion just right, a fine white powder blown off the palm into the face, you could slip into a fugue, passing for dead, the commentator said, a delicate art, folding in just the right amount of poison to shut down the body so no doctor could detect life, the victim wholly alert but unable to speak or move, a terrifying state. This happened to a Japanese businessman who ate a puffer fish, a delicacy in Japan, its liver the source of zombie poison, and found himself listening to doctors pronounce him dead. Cleaning the fish, apparently, required expertise. Only a little bit can kill or paralyze, and there's always the risk of waking up in a morgue or being buried alive. A commercial came on. Grace glanced over at Elwood, on his side now, still snoring. She pulled back the covers and got out of bed.

She walked onto the balcony. The tamarisk, bathed in moonlight, was still and silent. That's how they slept on warm nights, with the sliding glass door open instead of the air conditioner on, though she could hear the rattling of the others, grinding away, keeping bodies cool. People turned in early here, rising long before the noon heat.

She went back in. Now a witch doctor, a skinny man in a white shirt and billowy pants in a thick mangrove, was stopping here and there to pluck this or that leaf, explaining his potion's ingredients, and then from his pocket he pulled a small spotted fish shaped like a miniature whale—the infamous puffer fish. "From this," he said, "we extract the liver, grind it down, and mix it in, slip the powder into food or blow it. Like this." Palms up, he cupped hands together and blew. "This is the first step. Later we sneak back in the graveyard and dig them up, revive them with camphor. But if we wait more than twelve hours the person may suffocate." The scene shifted to a Haitian village, to an interview of an emaciated, sunken-eyed woman, a bright orange scarf wrapped around her hair, Mrs. Michaud, mother of a purported zombie, explaining how her son had died mysteriously and reappeared after he'd been buried. "We were in the market, and Paul said, 'Mama, I feel sick.' That night he died, and we buried him. Then day later someone saw him wandering in a neighboring village, so I went and found him, my son, alive but dead, and brought him home." But when a Haitian doctor tried to test the boy's blood to confirm it was her son, the boy kept slipping away until finally the doctor discovered the boy wasn't Paul Michaud or a zombie at all, but a homeless boy from another village, mildly retarded, abandoned by his parents. "This, the real story behind the zombies, is a sad one," the doctor said. "Wishful thinking. Mothers wanting their dead children back, and abandoned or lost children wanting mothers. So, they claim they are the dead risen—a delusion, perhaps not a bad one in a country as troubled as Haiti."

3

Three a.m. now, and he should have been in a deep sleep, beat from yesterday's driving, Bridgeport to Mono Lake to Sonora to see his father and back, but sleep had become complicated, a thing he desperately needed, a thing he dreaded. And there'd been a message on his answering machine when he'd gotten back from seeing his father, a man's voice, a French accent: "Mr. Uribe, this is Dr. LeBeau from the Inyo County Coroner's Office. It's urgent—" Stanley had cut the message short, though he should have expected it on the heels of Sheriff Boyd nabbing him at the lake, saying there was news, but still the sound of the doctor's voice had unnerved him.

In the kitchen now he put on a pot of coffee. He felt dull, hollow, his skull scooped out; worse, his stomach constantly gnawed at him, a chronic pressure at the notch of his ribs and the base of his throat. Had he forgotten to eat? Lying down only made it worse. Why couldn't people sleep on their feet like horses? Letting the coffee brew, Stanley sat on the couch in the dark watching his angel fish glide by, their striped bodies, long feelers, silky fins undulating from their bodies. *Pterophyllum scalare. Pterophyllum* meaning winged leaf, *scalare*, flight of stairs. He kept the tank light on so that they never saw night, lived in a perpetual state of fluid wakefulness. It was probably better that way since Mrs. Fisher was right—they didn't live long, and they kept him company while he waited for dawn.

He went back into the kitchen. He liked the smell of coffee, not so much the taste, but he poured himself a cup anyway and sat back down cradling it. This way he could pretend he was just rising with others, this a normal day, and that he wasn't the only one awake. Stretching his arms above his head, trying to loosen up his spine, open space between the discs, he thought maybe he had actually slept a little, and that was what was causing the pain. The head sharply turned on the pillow, the spine misaligned, would lead to trouble—Caitlin was right how stomach-sleeping would catch up with him. And then, after Lorna's death, his nightmare coming on so quickly after slipping into sleep, the same nightmare over and over. And the nightmare stuck with him all day, not just Lorna's body and the dark woods, but the dread. That's where it always started, in the dark woods, his headlights—not from his truck but his parents' station wagon, a Country Squire his parents drove when he'd been a kid—lighting up a patch of woods he didn't recognize, driving slowly down a dark road, searching for the right spot, Lorna laid out in the back. Stopping, he'd get out, go around and open the door, and pull her out feet first. That's how it was—every few minutes he'd drive to another spot, stop, pull her out, heave her over his shoulder like a deer, then slide her back in, drive on only to stop again, pull her out, then bring her back and drive some more. And each time he carried her, her arms dangling, hair flipped forward, he saw that place where her hair met her neck, crescent shaped, pale as a moon, and it was this that stuck with him the most, long after he'd woken, not her face—he never saw it—but the white of her neck, her red hair, and even in the dream he knew there would be no end to it, the futility of it—pulling her out, sliding her back in—and when he finally woke dread pinned him to his bed, a coffin he'd sunk into.

So each time the dream started up, he began waking himself, pushing the lid up, only to discover if he let himself drift off again that it would only start up again, so he simply avoided sleep, didn't tell anybody about it, not even Caitlin when she used to call or come over regularly right after Lorna had died to clean or cook as if he were an invalid. "Just the other day they brought in a fifteen-year-old in her pajamas, already in rigor, but the parents insisted we try to resuscitate her. You go to sleep and you don't wake up the next morning. It happens—even to kids," she'd said. It was her way of trying to snap him out of it, his funk, making death matter of fact. It was how she dealt with things, their baby, blood in the toilet.

Stanley put his coffee down and stood up now. Legs together, he bent forward, folding in half, his fingertips reaching for the floor, the nerves in the back of his legs screaming. Even if he got through the night, come morning the pain shot down his lower back and legs. Sleeping on his back or his side was impossible—he felt exposed, his hands got in the way. Where would he put them? And the cold got to him—the electric wall heater in his unit bust—especially his feet, and no amount of socks or blankets warmed them up, so now he paced, driving the blood down until he couldn't stand it any longer. He went in the bathroom, stripped, and then got in the shower. The hot water made his feet burn worse at first, but then his body began to relax, to come back to life, his feet defrosting, the blood circulating. Right before the hot water ran out, he stepped out and toweled off quickly, putting on sweats and socks and padding back into the kitchen where he poured himself more coffee before his body began to cool and the cold came back.

He sat down at the counter and contemplated sleep again, a dreamless sleep, a winged leaf floating. That's how all the commercials showed sleep if you just took the right pill. He peered at the angels gliding by beneath the purple neon light. Something was wrong. One was floating upside down. Funny, he hadn't noticed it before. He lifted the lid, slipped a net in, and scooped it out. With some you could tell, spots around the gills or they swam crooked before they went belly up. He shook the fish out of the net into a plastic bag. Then, lifting the bag up toward the tank light, he studied the fish again, its silky fins crumpled, feelers bent, and tossed the bag in the garbage. He grabbed his cup of coffee, but it had gone tepid. He peered into the living room at his bed, the rumpled blanket, the flat pillow, an old sleeper couch with coils that poked his ribs. It had come with the place, and he'd never bothered to toss it since he'd never planned to sleep on it. But after Caitlin had left, sleeping on it had become habit. The second floor, where the bedroom was, he'd abandoned, a lodger in his own house.

Stanley peered into the garbage at the dead fish between a milk carton and old spaghetti he'd tossed out earlier. He could always replace it. He looked over at the phone and then glanced at the door to the front office where he'd left the autopsy report. *Clad in dark gray pajamas and a light green floral top.* He'd seen her in those before, on the weekends when he visited, when Lorna slept late and hadn't bothered dressing. He rubbed one foot on top of the other, his feet already starting to get cold, and then slipped off his sweats, pulled on some jeans and boots, and grabbed his keys, going out through the office door. The cold air stung his face. At such a high altitude there were no warm nights. Hands in his pockets, he peered across 395 to The Bridgeport Bed & Breakfast, dark except for one window on the second floor, where, curtain pulled back, he saw someone. A woman maybe. And instinctively he crouched, feeling foolish. It was his motel, his place, after all. Hardly a criminal, he straightened up and looked back over at the window, but now it was dark, like all the others. What if he scrambled across, climbed up to the second floor, and knocked on her door? They could form a club—The All-Nighters or something like that.

Walking through the parking lot, light frost on windshields, he headed toward the back of his property instead, toward his own guest rooms, and stood on the stiff grass. He looked over to the rooms' sliding glass doors, lit globes glowing above each, worried someone might be awake, take him for a prowler.

As he headed down to the river, small rabbits, nibbling on the grass, scurried into the brush. Below the brush the Walker River ran—he could hear it—but it was buried too deep to see, so he looked up at the sky, hoping to spot the gauzy Milky Way, all the constellations, not that he could ever make any sense of them or even see them tonight, the half-moon too bright. He slid his hand in his pocket and fingered the ridges of his keys. He'd no business getting back on the road. He could hurt himself or someone else like the man he'd bought the motel from years ago; Russell Hayes II, or Rusty as he liked to be called—a scrawny, ponytailed guy with a crooked mouth and pocked skin—who, opening one door after another, had led him on an aimless tour of the motel, waggling the key as if it were a wand or a booze bottle, each room with the requisite chipped dresser, colorless prints, outdated TV, explaining how he'd inherited this "backwater" from his father while "the grand old dame," the Fielding Hotel in Berkeley, had gone to his brother. "That's why I got gypped," Rusty had said, laughing, "or maybe it's the other way around. I drink because I got gypped. You think that's fair?" And then he'd brought Stanley around to the pool, to the gate, saying in a teasing voice, "Not going to sell you this dump until you tell me the worst thing you've ever done." And before Stanley could say anything he'd said, "Okay. Me first. I once ran into a woman. Dark, rainy night. Poor visibility as they say. I'd had a few, of course. Glass, a thousand little pieces, and the rain coming through her windshield. Face cut up. Eyes open. The works."

Stanley turned away from the river and walked back up to the motel. Around front now, he stopped at the pool, peering into its empty shell, a crack he'd just patched for the coming season still visible. Stanley headed over to his truck, thinking maybe a short drive would tire him out, lull him like a baby, and then he'd turn back, slip into dreamless sleep, the kind that restores.

Lights on, he pulled onto 395. It was quiet, even the truckers off sleeping somewhere, and soon he was out of the town, into the forest, only the road's yellow lines and flashes of forest his high beams lit up. To break down here or pull someone over, as Sheriff Boyd once told him, inching up alongside a car, not knowing what's inside, would be spooky. Route 270. Bodie State Park. Stanley's lights flashed on the sign, the ghost town he'd described to the Fishers full of broken-down Gold Rush buildings where the settlers slept and you could peek in and see where life had been left. The last time he'd been there was with Lorna and Dell, and Dell, only five at the time, hadn't really cared where life had been left. It was the little gray rabbits scurrying along the paths, cutting their feet on the glass shards, litter left by the few who did visit, that concerned him.

Stanley rubbed his eyes and slowed down. Though he shouldn't, he turned onto 270 anyway and felt his tires mount the rough road, a road he'd only driven in daylight, and he remembered there were a lot of bends, but now the road seemed worse, terribly dark, darker than any place he'd ever been. He braked, put the truck into neutral, and sat there, idling, his high beams lighting the road ahead. He cranked up the heat; the warmth felt good. He looked in his rearview mirror, the dim red glow of his lights, knowing it was time to turn around, the road wide enough here, but the thought of his sad bed, the angels hovering in their purple watery world, the bitter coffee cold by now, the coroner's report tucked in his office drawer, *clad in dark gray pajamas*, made him shift again. Lurching forward, the truck took off, and he was moving again, even more swiftly, his eyes adjusting, patches of trees flashing before him as the wheel slid through his hands, the truck seeming to drive him, bouncing, lurching, turning bends, straightening itself out as if he were on some roller coaster. His heart pounding, he tried to pull back, lift his foot off the accelerator, but he was frozen, and he heard himself laugh, a sound he almost didn't recognize, the pain that had driven him out suddenly gone. He could have been anyone, going anywhere, on any planet. Nothing nagging at him. Just himself. A winged leaf. A solo star. Maybe he was hallucinating, the side effect of sleep deprivation. Maybe that's how the Fisher boy had felt out there at the Racetrack Playa, alone among the rocks blazing their own crazy trails. Craning his neck, Stanley tried to peer up through his windshield at that universe, to the other free-wheeling stars, but he couldn't see anything, the sky shut off, so he had to content himself with pieces of forest his headlights caught and then more trees and then a sign: Speed Limit 20 miles per hour. He pressed harder, the needle inching around until suddenly his headlights caught something else, and he braked hard, the truck straining back on itself. Antelope? Deer? In a clearing, three of them, eyes glowing, steam coming from their nostrils. Transfixed, Stanley sat there. One looming larger, an elaborate set of antlers spiraling from its head, stepped forward, its eyes glowing. Outrage? Disgust? Pity? Curiosity? Didn't all animals know what it was to be hunted, to have to run? Stanley caught himself in the rearview mirror, his shadowy face, the glint of his own eyes, and then he looked at the animal again. Exhaling, it finally turned and disappeared, the others following into the trees, and Stanley pulled his foot off the brake, and the truck lurched again, but soon the road would end, he knew, the dilapidated town would appear, and then what? He gripped the wheel tighter. Coming around another bend, he stopped short again, this time not because of any animal but a patch of woods he recognized not from his previous trip in with Lorna and Dell but from his dreams; these, the very woods he'd driven Lorna through nightly, dragging her in and out of the car, searching for the right spot to put her, and now, realizing his folly, how he'd driven himself full circle to the very place he'd run away from, realizing it was too late to back out, he pressed the accelerator even harder.

The next night Grace and Elwood ate dinner at the 49er Café, sitting at the L-shaped counter again, a kind of no man's land tucked at the back of the restaurant near the kitchen where mostly park staff ate. It had only been because of Jared's disappearance that they'd ended up there and not at a table like most tourists. That first year out, after that first phone call had come in, they'd flown into Vegas and driven into the park that night. Then after the sheriff had briefed them, explaining it was too dark to continue the search, they'd been taken over to the restaurant and led back by a sympathetic hostess to the counter so they could avoid the main dining room crowd. But now the counter had become more habit than hideout. Grace, swiveling around, looked over at the tables, at the families, listening to the collective chatter, the clink of glass and silverware, no longer dreading their curious glances, the sad pity of strangers; at least here in Death Valley where no one really lived, where most everyone, except the permanent employees, came and went, she no longer had to be brave, carry the mantle of hope that Jared would be found and all would be well. Too much time had passed. Only the Indian woman at the check-in counter took any interest, the updates from the sheriff's office having ended over a year ago. But still it did happen that cases suddenly came back to life, the phone rang, the missing miraculously found alive, this being the backdrop of every discussion in the grief therapy group about missing or dead children whose killer had not been found, and it was in this valley of doubt and hope, what the grief therapy group had come to call the Valley of Not Knowing or the VONK, that Grace now found herself: doubtful Jared was alive; hopeful he might be. She opened her menu. Badwater Burger, Scotty's Taco, Mushroom Rock Salad, Furnace Creek Sundae—the choices never changed, certainly no different than last night's. A waitress, a pale, broad-faced Nordic-looking girl with two blond pigtails, whom Grace hadn't seen before, came over with a pad in her hand. Her name tag said *Elsie from North Dakota.* "What can I get you folks tonight?"

Grace closed her menu. "The Panamint Chicken Burger." What she had last night. Little else was edible, though she'd tried once last year to order the Mesquite Pot Roast, but the waitress, an old-timer, one of the gray women that worked the counter every year they'd been there, had, with a sad look of pity, as promptly as she delivered it, taken it back, mumbling, "Not even fit for coyotes."

"And you, sir?"

"Badwater Burger with fries."

A minute later, the young waitress returned with drinks, a cup of hot tea for Grace and iced tea for Elwood. Pulling out a straw from her apron, she said, matter of factly, "Most tourists hate the counter, but it's better that way, isn't it? Here instead of out there. All the noise. Everybody happy." She nodded over Grace's head, toward the tables. "Anyway, your food will be up in a jiffy."

Grace dipped her tea bag into the hot water and then poured sugar in, watching the granules dissolve. Always curious about the staff here, the enclave where they lived, a small swath of land adjacent to the stables hidden by a thick border of tamarisk trees, she watched the waitstaff, all kids or retirees, pick up their orders and rush to deliver them.

Lifting his glass, Elwood took a long drink. "Parched," he said.

"It is the desert," Grace said.

Elwood swiveled in his chair. "I like the way they renovated this place."

"I like the booths better. They should have left them." She looked up at the ceiling. "Same fans, though. Floor's just as creaky. Counter's the same."

"Counter's always the same. You know I've always wanted to wear one of those chef hats, the big, tall puffy ones."

Grace looked over at the kitchen, at the two chefs working over the griddle. "Why? They seem kind of silly. What if they caught fire? Look, I was just thinking about Jared's car, if we'll ever get it back."

"I don't know. It's evidence, right? Why? You plan to drive it?"

"I guess one of us would have to get it home."

"I mean as your own car."

"Me? A 1950s Cougar. Purple. No, we'd just drive it every once in a while to keep it running."

"I still can't figure out how he got it out there, a low rider like that," Elwood said.

"He was always a good driver, was careful. He loved that car. There's no way he'd leave it."

"Here we go." The waitress slid their plates on the counter. "One Panamint. One Badwater. Anything else I can get you?"

Elwood lifted his bun, peering underneath. "Looks all there."

Grace looked down at her food, at the open-faced chicken seared horizontally and glistening, beside it a neat mound of potato salad, parsley sprinkled on top. She lifted her fork and then put it down. Elwood looked at her plate. "What?"

"I don't think I can."

"Looks better than usual."

"You say that every year."

"Well, you get the same thing every year. Maybe you should order something different. It's only the second night here. You can't be sick of the food already."

"It's my stomach." She pressed her hand to her abdomen.

Chewing, he wiped his mouth and looked at her. "You're

turning into a ghost."

"Well, this ghost is going back to the room and lie down a bit. Get my food to go. I'll try to eat it later." She slid off her chair.

"I'll get mine to go too."

"No, it'll get cold. You stay."

"But it's dark out."

"Something wrong?" Their waitress had reappeared, brow furrowed.

"No." Grace glanced down at her plate. "It's what I ordered."

"No good?" The girl studied the plate.

"If you could just wrap it up."

"She's not feeling well," Elwood said, as the waitress lifted the plate.

"Don't rush, Elwood." Grace got up. "I'll be fine." She walked up the aisle, past the crowded tables, dodging a waitress carrying a food tray. Outside she walked along the veranda and then down the steps onto the road, the one that led back to the motel. Had she really been sick she would have cut across the grassy area, past the pool, to the room; however, she'd decided before the meal to take a different route back without Elwood, a route he would have disapproved of, through the employee enclave on foot, at eye level, in the anonymity of darkness, not from a park helicopter as they had that first year out in daylight with rangers flying across the miniature city of rising palms, trailers and bungalows, and all the stuff in between—lawn chairs, bicycles, tires, garbage cans.

Now, poised in the dark, at the border between the Ranch grounds and the enclave—an invisible one since no sign marked it—Grace saw an odd sight, what looked like a remnant of a lost planet, but nearing it she realized it was nothing more than a half-built cinderblock wall, a lit-up soda machine against it, but still she shuddered, even though it was warm and she was only minutes from the restaurant and her room, thinking how easy it would be to go back, to rejoin Elwood at the counter, eat her food. She'd always been careful not one to wander off in the dark alone, and she didn't like lying. What if something happened to her? And, after all, did she really think such a trek would rid herself of the VONK, the valley of not knowing? And was this what the VONK looked like—trailers, palm trees, and junk? Harmless stuff, how people lived. Wasn't she being as naive as the doctor's wife and all the other women from the grief therapy group who'd gone to the psychic? In their kitchens over coffee, slipping each other crystal ball-adorned business cards, they'd played back their tape, the psychics always saying the same things, asking the same questions: *I could be wrong but I'm seeing... Has so and so ever...? I'm seeing a tiny ball of yarn unraveling* while the grieving mother wept, saying, *Yes. Yes.*

Grace started walking again, trying to adjust her eyes to the dark. Cutting through the enclave, looping back to the motel, a minor five-minute detour, was her plan. Then it would be over, out of her system. Past the soda machine now, she entered the enclave and, turning right, headed down a street of bungalows and trailers. Oddly enough, even in the dark, something was familiar about the place, maybe from a dream she'd often had about being stranded on a dark street. Or maybe a passage from one of Jared's Castaneda books, the one about a young man deep in the desert at night trying to find his way home. Having just left a party, heading down a dark path, he spots a crouching figure ahead and, leery, wonders if he should turn back, rejoin the party. But he keeps going, hoping it's only a shadow, a bush, a friendly person resting, but as he passes, the figure starts to unfurl, chasing him, a giant bird, a roadrunner, zigzagging madly behind him.

Grace took a deep breath and kept walking. Up ahead small triangular flames danced in the air, and there was movement, the outlines of people beneath a canopy or tent. Then she heard a voice, a man's voice, echoing through the dark. "Hey!" In the distance a figure was standing up, arms waving. "Come on and join the party." Grace stood motionless in the dark, wondering if the man had mistaken her for someone else. He called out again. "You lost?" And when she didn't answer and started walking again, hoping to pass, he shouted again, "Do you speak?"

"No," she shouted, "I mean I'm not lost." Her voice wavered, the sound of it traveling through the dark. She wanted to keep moving, get back to the motel, but she hung there, unsure.

"Well, then, why don't you come over here and have a beer before the coyotes get you?" He laughed and then there was more laughter, the high, bell-like laughter of a woman.

Grace had seen her share of coyotes in the park, scrawny, hungry things loping across barren landscape, eyeing her warily. They liked to pick off campers' dogs, the little tied-up ones that couldn't defend themselves. She started walking again, but then, just when she thought she'd gotten out of range, someone stepped out of the dark and stood beneath a florescent streetlight, a woman, barefoot, in a T-shirt and shorts, cutoffs frayed at the bottom, a beer bottle in her hand. She was smiling shyly, head cocked to the side. "Lost, are you?" she said, looping her hair behind her ear.

"I'm staying at the Ranch," Grace said.

"The lost ones usually wind up clear out on the Indian reservation. Even darker out there. Lions too, though no one's ever seen one. Suffocate their prey." She stepped closer to the light and drank from the bottle. "Anyway, no one's ever been attacked here before." She shrugged her shoulders, then sat down on the curb. Lifting the bottle, she pointed it at Grace. "Say, I've seen you before. You famous? A lot of Hollywood types come here."

Grace shook her head.

"Yeah, I guess the stars mostly stay up at the Inn. But I've seen you before."

"You've probably seen a lot of people before," Grace said.

She laughed. "Funny. Oh, now I've got it. The lady with the disappeared son. Quite a while ago, right? Saw you on TV. We keep track here, the long-term workers, the lifers, you know."

Grace nodded, surprised the woman remembered, no less recognized her in the dark.

"That German family with two children vanished over ten years ago. They just found their van in the backcountry. The kids' shoes still on the dashboard. Really sad."

"A family?"

"Candy bar wrappers and water bottles. Petrified poop under rocks. They were there for a while. Tires fine. No reason to die. Drive in. Drive out. Or maybe they got lost. Or wanted to die. You know, all these years, I've never been out to the Racetrack Playa where yours disappeared. Hardly anyone I know has. That road eats tires. I hear they charge a lot for a tow."

"Is that where they found that family, at the Racetrack?"

"Some other part of the park, a place with no name."

"It's the wind," Grace said.

"What?"

"And rain at the Racetrack that move the rocks, and the rocks leave tracks."

"Oh yeah, I hear it's one giant Ouija board."

"Hey, what's going on out there?" the man called. "Party's over here. Beer's getting warm."

"Oh, shut up, Vance! We're having a conversation here. Just us women."

"Is that your husband?" Grace asked.

The woman laughed. "Vance? God no. Works at the gas station."

"Well," Grace said, "I won't keep you."

"You're not keeping me," the woman said. "Am I keeping you?"

"My husband—he'll be—" Grace said.

"I'm coming to get you." From the dark the man called out again in a sing-song voice.

The woman laughed. "You don't need to worry about him. Drunk is all."

"What do you do here?" Grace asked.

"Clean. The 600 building. The one you never stay in. That's why you don't see me. Maybe someday I'll get bumped up to the 800 building. Better views. Fewer slobs. Something to look forward to." She lifted the bottle and drank from it. "Sure, you don't want some?"

Grace glanced at her watch, even though it was too dark to see it.

"Your husband. Right. I forgot." She rose to her feet. Walking backward out of the light, she said, "See, I'm disappearing," in a mock cartoonish voice as if she'd swallowed helium.

Grace started walking more quickly now, the voice reminding her of the boy who'd sent his mother an eerie tape of himself, a joke his mother had thought, in his dorm room, sliding off a chair onto the floor, laughing hysterically, signing off "I'm dying" in a comic, helium-fueled voice. A week later his roommate found him hanging. These were the sorts of stories told in the grief therapy group, newcomers describing that first moment of panic, that call coming in, just as Grace's had, hers on a sunny day, pulling her in from backyard weeding, and a foreign voice, flat and official-sounding, a man identifying himself from the Inyo County Sheriff's Department: "Mrs. Fisher, is your son at home? Has he contacted you? Do you know where he is? Where would he have gone?" He'd peppered her with questions before she could catch her breath, and bewildered, she'd wondered if Jared had done something wrong. Spring break could make even a good kid go bad. Speeding? Drinking? A prank gone too far? Until it struck her that something had happened to *him*, and she felt herself stiffen, the phone slip from her hand.

Ahead, in the distance, she saw the stable lights and heard a horse whinny. The early evening wind brought the smell of hay and manure. She picked up her pace, passing the stables, where the horses were feeding, then cut across the parking lot. Climbing up the outer steps of her building, she stopped short. A coyote, on its hind legs, was eating out of the garbage. Lifting its head, it peered at her, eyes iridescent. The golf course coyote. She knew the animal, had seen it loping across the golf course the past two years, well fed and used to people, not one of those desperate, dog-snatching scrawny ones. Grace, backing down the steps, hurried around the building, worried that Elwood had beaten her back, and entered from the other side. Down the hallway, at her room, she slid her card in and opened the door.

The room was dark and warm. She turned on the lights and the ceiling fan, and then opened the sliding door. Then she pulled off her shoes and lay on the bed. She glanced at the clock. Where was Elwood? And then she remembered the coyote. She lifted the phone, but then cradled it. Who was she going to call? The animal would probably be long gone before any ranger got there. From the nightstand she lifted the book she'd bought at the ranger station earlier in the day, on its cover a roadrunner, its gold-ringed eye glaring out the side of its head. She'd seen these birds here in Furnace Creek shooting across the road between the pool and the date grove, queer-looking with a crazy tuft of feathers springing from its head, thick legs, and a long neck stretching for a finish line. Grace flipped to a random page:

> Lore has it that the intrepid roadrunner doesn't limit it-self to lizards but takes on tarantulas. Though the road-runner can sprint over twenty miles per hour, it takes its time killing, crippling the spider by tearing off one leg after another. Then, to tenderize it, the roadrunner whips it against a rock and then devours it. Rumor has it roadrunners also take on rattlers, flinging them up onto prickly cacti, impaling them.

The door opened.

Grace sat up and said, "There you are. Did you see the coyote at the garbage can? What took you so long?"

Elwood opened the small fridge and slid a box in. "I got a book at the general store. One of those Indian mysteries. That's all they sell. Not too bad, but they all end the same way. How's your stomach?"

Grace picked up her book again. "These roadrunners, they beat their food to death before swallowing it. Did you know that?"

Elwood sat down on the bed and lifted the book out of her hands, looking at the cover. "Well, they're supposed to be ornery. Even hate themselves, pecking at their own reflections. That's what a ranger told me."

Grace looked over at herself in the mirror above the dresser, trying to imagine it, pecking at herself over and over, cracking glass. The roadrunner, of course, just thought it was another roadrunner.

On the other bed, Elwood sat down and opened his book while Grace put hers down and picked up the Manson book and opened it up at the center where pictures of the girls he recruited were, blurry black-and-white mug shots, disheveled hair, young, sullen faces, looking back at her, and then, turning the page, she started reading.

Elwood looked over at her. "Don't you ever start at the beginning? Roadrunners. Manson. No wonder your stomach's upset. You should try one of these murder mysteries. At least they're not real, and they always catch the bad guys."

"Well, they catch them here too. But this is strange." She flipped back in the book to a paragraph she'd marked. "Says here Manson had his people digging holes all over the desert looking for some kind of Nirvana, a land of plenty, food and wine. If they could just find the entrance, then they'd be saved."

"Saved from what?"

Grace shrugged. "I don't know. Helter skelter. The end of the world or something like that. I have to keep reading."

4

Stanley woke in a sweat, the sheets damp beneath his back. Someone was calling his name. Was it Cody? Had he overslept? Opening his eyes, he tried to focus on what was before him, his gaze landing on the contour of a chin, a round Band-Aid on it, its center dark where blood had pooled, and then lower to a set of hands, thick red fingers wrapped around a silver rail. Then he heard a whooshing sound and turned his head. There he saw a man in a bed, a tube snaking into his mouth, his head shuddering a little each time the whoosh came. On the other side of him was a window, light pouring in. The image of his own windshield, the dark glint, flashed in his mind. "Stanley?" The voice brought his eyes back to the person it belonged to, the face hovering directly above him, broad and ruddy.

"Sheriff Boyd here. Doc said you've been in and out of it all day. Might have some amnesia, so I won't stay long. Wouldn't be here if it wasn't important, even more important now that you nearly killed yourself. Remember what we talked about the other day at the cemetery, at Mono Lake? Or maybe you don't." He held up a folder. "See this? Pictures here the coroner wants you to see." He put the folder on the nightstand. "They might not make sense, but you're to look at them anyway and call the coroner soon as you're recovered. "Understand?" He leaned over a little closer. Stanley could feel his breath on his face. "Stanley, you know who I am?" Then, straightening up, he cleared his throat. "Like I said before, there are developments. Important ones. Otherwise I wouldn't be here. So look at these when you're ready." He straightened up and walked toward the door and then turned back around as if he'd forgotten something, mouth opening and closing like a fish, a large grouper Stanley once had, and then was gone. Stanley, turning his head toward the nightstand, reached for the folder, but suddenly he felt nauseous and everything went black.

When he woke again, a series of beeps were piercing the air, and Stanley turned toward the other bed, but soon the beeping stopped, and Stanley rolled his head back to the nightstand where the folder still sat. Nausea gone for the moment, he tried for the folder again, surprised by all the wires running up his arm, a thick needle taped in the fold. The folder just out of reach, he felt around the bed for the controller—all hospital beds had them—and raised the bed back. Then he tried again, this time grasping it, laying it on his lap. Outer space. That's how the first picture looked, satellite images of planets—a collage of gray, white spaces, and black specks. Sifting through the other pages, he blinked his eyes, trying to bring them into focus. He glanced at the man in the bed beside him again and then turned back to the picture before him, which to his surprise started taking shape—petroglyphs of buffalo, fox, sheep. On another page a great sea turtle turned toward him, its large pensive eye set in a gray socket, dry, withered skin of its craned neck veined white, embedded into a backdrop of gray stone streaked white and speckled with small black ovals. Yet the turtle was no stone but rather in motion, its eye looking right at him. Blurriness and clarity, stillness and motion, all the pictures, as he flipped through them, had that peculiar quality, like looking at artifacts beneath a microscope sunk in several feet of water. Was he hallucinating? He looked over at the doorway. Doctors and nurses passing, a man pushing a mop, paused, calling over to him, "Hey, man, glad to see you awake!" He continued flipping through the pages, pausing at one, a small sailboat trapped in a gale, thrust up on a steep swell, teetering at the top of a rising wall of water. Which way would he fall—backward into a churning sea bottom or plummet over the top into a shallow reef wrapped around a sandbar, in it a hybrid creature half lizard, half prong-horned sheep, and the more ordinary lobster, goldfish, sea snake, and a wayward swordfish waiting out the storm? And then he focused on the sailboat itself, white with a tall black sail, on it a tiny figure, really just a gray line, a slash of something that might be a man clinging to the mast. Then he felt the pages slip out of his hand, his eyes shut, and when he opened them again he gasped. Towering over him was another man—tall, emaciated, white-clad, slightly stooped—the Frozen Man from *The Sonora*!

"No need to be frightened, Mr. Uribe. I'm Dr. Katz. Your doctor. You're in Sonora General. I've been taking care of you. You've been slipping in and out of consciousness all day. But your vitals are good. No organ damage. Do you know why you're here?"

The river running, rabbits scurrying, Lorna's red hair, the deer in his headlights—he looked down at his feet beneath the white sheet and wiggled them. At least the sensation, the cold burn, was no longer there.

"Well, don't worry, memory loss is normal. In time it may come back. You have a mild concussion, some bruised ribs, the sort of injuries that heal. Your face is a railroad track right now, but you should have minimal scaring. Eventually no one will know any different."

"Who found me?"

"A caretaker from Bodie, I understand, driving out to buy supplies. On the road. You'd likely been there several hours. You were airlifted out. Your wife's been up a lot. On her breaks. Said she never saw you sleep so soundly. The sheriff too. He left that folder." The doctor lifted it off his chest and put it back on the nightstand. "I'm sorry about your sister. Sheriff Boyd told me what happened. I understand there's news though."

"I didn't try to kill myself."

"No one said you did."

"My sister didn't either."

"No one said she did."

Stanley glanced over at the man in the bed beside him again, and the doctor, following his gaze, said, "Car accident like you. Less fortunate though. We've been trying to wean him off the vent."

"Those loud beeps."

"Means his oxygen is low, and the ventilator has to adjust.

Nothing to worry about. The machine will breathe for him."
He reached over and pulled the curtain between the beds. "If
you continue to improve, we may release you as soon as tomorrow afternoon. Your wife said she'd get you home."

Grace heard a knock at the door.

A stocky man in a greasy jumpsuit, a spray of salt and pep-
per hair combed over his head, stood before her. "You the folks
that need the jump?" he asked.

Grace eyed the name stitched on his jumpsuit and felt
herself stiffen. It couldn't be, she thought, as she recalled last
night's foray, the long-haired woman saying, *Oh, that's Vance. He
works at the gas station.* Grace shook her head and sighed. Just her
luck their car wouldn't start this morning.

"Mrs. Fisher?"

"Yes, thanks, we'll be right down." She closed the door.

"That the gas station?" Elwood asked, coming out of the
bathroom.

"I think so."

Elwood chuckled. "You're not sure?"

Grace put on her sunglasses. "It's him."

They went downstairs and walked across the parking lot.
The gas station truck was parked there. "Which one are you?"
the man asked.

Elwood pointed. "Over there."

"I'll just pull over, and we'll jump her. Then you'll follow me
back to the gas station."

"How long will it take?" Elwood asked.

"Depends if I have a battery that fits." He got in his truck
and pulled it alongside their car, then started attaching the cables.

"Maybe you should wait in the room," Elwood said, opening
the car door. "Then, if he's got a battery, I'll swing back and we
can head out to the Ubehebe Crater."

"If we can't go today, we can both go tomorrow. Crater's the
first stop on the tour."

"The tour?"

"Desert Adventures," Grace said. "Remember before we left we talked about going back out to the Playa. It's been two years."

Elwood sighed. "That's not going to bring Jared back. Isn't that what we decided?"

"Okay, she's all ready to go." The man, out of his truck again, pulled the cables and let their hood down with a bang. "Now just follow me over."

"So what do you want to do?" Elwood asked, opening the car door.

"Go on the tour tomorrow."

"No, I mean about this gas station. The man's not going to wait all day."

Grace looked over at the idling truck, thinking even if he did recognize her she could just say she'd gotten lost. She couldn't have been the only one, the lone pioneer who'd lost her way. She walked around the car and got in. "What if he doesn't have the right battery?"

"Well, maybe we'll get lucky. At least there's a gas station here. Help. People. Out there on your tour you won't be so lucky." Elwood started following the truck through the lot.

"It's not like we're the Donner Party, Elwood. The driver carries a satellite phone."

Elwood turned onto the main road and then took another quick left into the gas station, pulling up near the pumps while the truck parked beside the garage. "If he can't fix it in time, we'll just stay put today, do something different, try the food at the Inn. We can walk up there. It's not that far."

From her window Grace watched the man rummage through shelves of boxes.

"And we can walk around the grounds," Elwood said. "Remember that movie with the alcoholic guy and the prostitute in Las Vegas where he drinks himself to death? At the pool and the waiter brings them over glasses and vodka on a silver platter and everything breaks? That was filmed at the Inn."

"Here he comes," Grace said.

"What was his name?"

"The gas station attendant?" Grace asked.

"No, the alcoholic guy—the actor?"

"Sorry, folks. No dice," the man said, leaning into Grace's window. "Pahrump's the closest town. Not too far from Vegas. Your best shot." He wiped his forehead with a handkerchief.

"What if the engine dies?" Grace said, hoping her sunglasses would disguise her.

"Won't happen as long as you keep moving and don't take any detours. Only folks that get lost go where they don't belong. Long as you keep the car running you'll be fine. The Mrs. need not worry. Consider it your little adventure." Smiling, he winked at her, and she looked out the windshield to an empty picnic table beside the road, a palm tree above it.

"What about Panamint Springs?" Elwood said. "The gas station there?"

"They'll have even less than we do, and then you'll have to go to Ridgecrest or Bishop then deadhead back, an even longer drive."

"We better go, Elwood," Grace said. She started rolling up her window, but the man put his hand on top of it and with the other pointed toward the road. "Hold on now, folks. Stay on the road. No shortcuts, and you'll be fine." The man straightened up and stepped back.

Elwood raised his hand. "Thank you. Appreciate it." He pulled away, easing onto the road.

Grace, looking into the side mirror, watched the man start to shrink away.

"Nice fellow," Elwood said. "Didn't even charge us. Good thing you came along. I think he liked you."

"Whatever you do, Elwood, don't stop."

"Nothing's going to happen, Grace. We have plenty of gas. Plenty of daylight. You heard what he said."

As they came around a bend the flagstone and white stucco Inn came into view, perched up on a hill, its ceramic-tiled roof orange against the blue sky, a line of tall palms flanking its long veranda.

"So I don't remember. How did it end—that movie?" Grace asked.

"In Vegas in some dive motel. The guy's in bed. He opens his eyes, sees the sun rising, and dies. Hey, look how crowded Golden Canyon is."

Grace glanced over to the lot, to the mustard-colored mouth of the canyon, people milling around it, an outhouse nearby. "I don't see the point of it. I mean if you're going to kill yourself, why not do it quickly? Why make a movie about it and expect people to watch it?"

"I'd think you'd like that kind of movie, a guy refusing help, deciding to live his life his own way. Die his own way. Not your usual feel-good movie."

"I never said therapy was bad for everyone."

Elwood slowed down. Ahead a few cars were waiting to turn in to Artist's Palette, a popular drive up a steep, colorful canyon. "Nicolas Cage. That was his name, the actor."

"The salt flats are coming up," Grace said, as Elwood looped around another bend, the road starting to drop. "Too bad we can't stop." Up ahead Grace could see Badwater's stark white beach, almost blinding beneath the clear blue sky. Shielding her eyes, she peered down the long stretch of the beach flattened by all the foot traffic, far out to the spot most people turned back, where the beach became crusty, the salt rising up into octagons. Last spring she'd strayed that far out, thinking the other side—where the mountains began and what looked like a cabin of sorts stood—wasn't that far, but the desert really did play tricks and soon enough she'd realized she would never reach that cabin—if there was one at all. Still, she understood the draw, how easily you could be pulled out.

"Let's stop here on the way back," Elwood said.

"Whatever you do, Elwood, don't stop. Not now."

"It's not stopping that's the problem, Grace. As long as the engine keeps running. Plus, we're still in civilization, plenty of cars on the road. Once we get to the outskirts of the park, though, well, there won't be much of anything, just that Amargosa Opera House with the lady in the red slippers."

"Who?"

"She used to dance there. She and her husband were driving through and got a flat. That's how she discovered the old theater and they decided to buy it and refurbish it. She painted people on the walls, a fake audience, until real people came to see her dance. Anyway, it should be coming up. A small motel there too. Haunted."

"I had no idea," Grace said. "How do you know all this?"

"You're not the only one that reads. Here we go," Elwood said. "I think it's right past this ranger booth." No one in it as they passed through.

Then they came upon two windswept, faded adobe buildings, one with numbered doors and another windowless with one large entryway, *The Amargosa Opera House* painted across it, and an empty, sand-covered parking lot.

"So where are the people?" Grace asked.

"She retired. Danced until she was eighty-eight."

"Well, it must have been lonely out here for her."

After driving several miles, they passed a faded sign. "Welcome to Pahrump." Then a barbed-wire fence separating road from land started. Newspaper, bottles, tires, shoes, a plastic baby doll littered the shoulder.

"Well, at least there's no dead dogs," Grace said. The car lurched. She pressed her hand to the dashboard.

"Sorry," Elwood said. "Pothole city, but at least it's not Racetrack Road."

Up ahead Grace saw houses, ranch-style, washboard roads leading out to them, some abandoned-looking, windows smashed in, shards hanging down like fangs. "Looks like Trona," she said, "minus the factory and the smell."

"There's an Indian casino somewhere in town, I think," Elwood said.

"I wonder if snakes hole up in there, in those abandoned ones."

"Snakes?" Elwood asked.

"There was a story in the newspaper about a man who

cleaned out foreclosed homes in Florida. He opens the fridge and out springs a snake, a cottonmouth."

Elwood started to slow down again, up ahead an intersection and another sign: Pahrump, Population 36,441. Elwood turned. "Here we go," he said. They passed a Mobile Station, McDonald's, Safeway, Walmart but few cars on the road itself.

"Looks like a holiday here," Grace said. "Think this place is going to be open?"

Elwood pointed out his windshield to the towering sign for the Happy Go Lucky Casino, its large lot all parked up.

"So that's where everyone is. I should have known," Grace said.

"Well, not everyone, I hope," Elwood said. "Let's hope someone's working." Elwood turned left into The Pahrump Auto Shop, a small cement building with four parking spots in front, one taken.

"You better leave the car running. Go in first and see if they have the right battery. In case we have to drive to Vegas." Grace watched Elwood walk through the door to the counter; then he came back out along with another man in a blue jumpsuit who slid into the driver's seat. Grace got out, and the man backed the car out.

"It'll take about half an hour," Elwood said, squinting in the sun. "I'm going to wait inside. Kind of hot out here. Want to come in?"

"I'm going to grab a newspaper and wait out here." She liked the heat. Air conditioning made her shiver. She walked down to the sidewalk and slid two quarters in the slot and pulled out a *Pahrump Voice*, then walked back up into the lot and sat on a curb. She opened the newspaper turning through the pages, scanning the headlines: "Nevada Round-Up of Wild Horses Protested"; "Kamchatkan Residents Eaten by Bears"; "The Giants of Death Valley"; "Woman Kills Herself, Buyers Converge on House"; "Bones Found in Remote Area of Death Valley":

> Bones found in Devastation Canyon have now been confirmed to be Beatrice Freling, a so-called follower

of the late writer Carlos Castaneda. An anthropologist, he became known for several wildly popular 1970s books about a shaman named Don Juan. After retiring from writing, Castaneda lived his later years in seclusion in LA, where he developed a small following of devoted fans. Freling, one of a trio of women reported to be especially close to him, apparently lived in his house and led meditation workshops on his behalf. Deputy Sheriff Clive Sweeny said Freling was dressed in a blouse, a denim skirt, and sandals and was clutching one of Castaneda's books when hikers found her remains. "It's possible," he said, "she intended to take a hike and strayed off trail, losing her bearings. Or maybe she never intended to come back." After Castaneda died of cancer two years ago, his followers believed he would ignite into a whirlwind of flame, shooting up into the night sky. When this didn't happen, the group largely disbanded, and the trio of women, including Freling, disappeared. The other two women have never been found.

Alongside the story was a picture of Castaneda's house, an attractive two-story stucco with a tile roof and palm trees around it. Grace glanced back at the shop where she could see Elwood inside at the counter and then turned back to a passing car, a little boy, face pressed to the window, peering down at her. She started reading another story.

In the middle of the night while they slept a family of four in a small mining village in northern Kamchatka were killed and eaten by a pack of brown bears. These bears, some of the largest in the world, can grow to a massive fifteen feet tall, weigh up to 1800 pounds, and run an astonishing thirty-five miles per hour. Endangered and normally reclusive, they prefer to feast at the region's salmon-rich rivers; however, drought and a dwindling salmon population have forced the bears into the villages where terrified locals have little means to defend themselves. Village Mayor Oleg Savin said, "Bears who eat people will eat people again." Rescinding the country's hunting ban, Igor Petrov, secretary of the interior, has dispatched biologists and hunters to the village.

She turned the page.

Early gold prospectors Reginald Tuffin and Jed Stully claimed to have fallen down a chute into a room of giants, finding four mummified men some ten-feet tall seated at a ruby-studded table. The stunned prospectors said that the foursome were holding goblets, presumably of wine, when some catastrophe befell them, leading to their sudden death mid-toast. Tuffin and Stully, who apparently pried one of the goblets out of a mummy's hand, assured journalists they would be donating it to the famed Museum of Natural History. But then the prospectors, unable to produce the goblet, disappeared, and the incident was labeled a hoax. However, Paiute legend does give some credence to the possibility of a Death Valley underworld, the *Shin-Au-Av*, the repository of the dead. A chief, the story goes, mourning his wife's death, searches underground, coming to a bridge over an abyss where he has to fight demons to cross. Once across he finds a lovely land of spirits eating and dancing around a blazing fire, and there he spots his wife. Overjoyed, he starts to lead her out. But the spirits warn them not to look back, and his wife, torn between her spirit life and her husband, does, evaporating in his arms.

"All done," Elwood said.

Grace stood up.

"Anything interesting?"

"Man-eating bears and happy spirits beneath Death Valley." Grace closed the newspaper and got up.

"No wonder Manson was digging holes."

Grace saw their car pull up alongside the building.

The man got out. "Can stop anywhere you like now. Vegas or wherever."

"We're headed back to Death Valley," Grace said.

"I hear it's nice there. Been meaning to go." He lifted his hand. "Well, have a good trip."

"That's astonishing," Grace said, getting in, laying the news-paper on her lap.

"Let's do air for a while," Elwood said. "Then we'll roll down the windows."

Grace closed her vents. "To live so close."

"Happens all the time. The closer it is, the less likely you are to see it." Elwood placed his hand on the back of Grace's seat, and, looking over his shoulder, started to back out. "Cold system's moving in over the next few days. Heard it on the radio inside. Snow at the high elevations. Mammoth Lakes is sup-posed to get half a foot. Some at the Charcoal Kilns. No way that tour outfit's going to make it out to the playa tomorrow. It's much farther away than the crater and up higher. You probably don't remember, on that road out, because it's so rough, how high up it goes."

"I'm sure they'll cancel the tour if it snows. Who ever heard of getting trapped in a snowstorm in Death Valley?"

"Telescope Peak sometimes has snow all year round. Either way, you don't have to go. What do you expect to find out there anyway?"

"I just want to see it again, under different conditions, in my right mind."

"In your right mind?"

"We were both in a panic then. We saw everything and noth-ing. Why don't you just come with me? Crater's the first stop, then the Racetrack. I'm sure it's not too late to book another seat."

"If you can't remember something, it's probably because you're not meant to."

"Yes, that makes sense if something horrible happened to me."

"Something horrible did happen to you, Grace."

Grace sighed. In the past she'd allowed herself to be lulled into such complacency, had even thought of starting her own support group or anti-support group, Victimhood No More or the VNM. She'd become fond of acronyms. It seemed every support group had one. "All those well-wishers coming up the driveway, ringing our doorbell, women with their Bundt cakes. Perfect strangers. Their contorted faces. I don't understand that."

"So, you think Jared is dead? You've given up?"

Grace shrugged. "I didn't say that. I don't know." She opened the newspaper again to Castaneda's house, her eye landing on an upstairs window, a shadowy face cloistered behind it, and then she closed it again.

"Well, people talk," Elwood said. "Remember we wanted publicity. Did you really think you could have it both ways? It seems to me people are just being kind. They don't know what to do, so they say too much or nothing at all. You think people look down on you? That you're marked in some way? Are you sure this isn't all the result of your own self-pity? You don't like being treated like a victim but you act like one anyway."

Grace flinched. That wasn't what she'd intended, though she wouldn't deny that at her most bitter, she'd found herself eyeing strangers, wondering why they got to amble down the sidewalk on a sunlit day while others lay buried in a box, muffled and silent. "That's just the thing, Elwood. This isn't about me or you or anyone else. My family. Your family. Friends. Other grieving parents. The people that carry their dead children on their backs, strangers that want some piece of that. It's about Jared, the ones no longer here. We have to keep reminding ourselves of that."

"Well, I still don't think you should go on that tour. You'll go out there and then…" Elwood said.

"What?"

"Nothing."

"Nothing?"

"You'll find nothing and then what? You don't want sympathy. You don't want to be ignored."

"Why don't you just come with me?"

"I don't see the point in being disappointed."

"Elwood, you don't need to worry about me." Grace peered out at the empty houses they'd passed on their way in, the dark squares and ragged glass.

Sighing, Elwood looked up through the windshield. "It's awfully clear now. Well, maybe the storm won't come in."

5

Cleared for release, Stanley stood beside the bed of his hospital roommate, a young man maybe in his twenties or early thirties with fine brown hair and a pale boyish face. Other than the shuddering of his head, he was perfectly still, a bluish cast beneath his eyes. No one had visited him, except the doctor, as far as he knew. Stanley reached down to touch his hand but pulled back, fearing it might be cold or that his touch might somehow distress the man, sending the machine into a beeping fit. So instead he rested his hands on the bed rail and said, "Hey, when you wake up call me," and then glanced back at the door, fearing a passing nurse might rush in, admonish him. "No charge," he spoke more softly, "and it's beautiful where I live." From his wallet he pulled an old business card, on it a simple sketch of the Walker River snaking through brush and put it on the nightstand. "Rabbits there too, and if you're lucky a bear." He heard a sound behind him and turned.

"Oh, Mr. Uribe," Dr. Katz said, "I thought you were already gone. Your wife's picking you up, isn't she?"

Stanley turned back to the man. "You think he can hear us?"

Dr. Katz stepped up beside Stanley. "Patients unconscious longer have said they could. They just can't respond. Like being trapped at the back of a cave—that's how one of my patients described it. He could see the light but just couldn't reach it. You, on the other hand, I expect to fully recover, though you may have some temporary memory loss, some residual headaches." Dr. Katz reached out his hand. "I wish you the best, Mr. Uribe, that you finally get an answer about your sister." Then turning, he left the room, and Stanley, grabbing the folder and a pill bottle from the nightstand, followed. Downstairs, the doors parted, and he walked out and got into Caitlin's car.

"What took so long?" she asked.

"Dr. Katz thinks you're my wife." He put on his seat belt.

"Well, technically I am," she said, pulling out.

"You want me to sign the papers?"

"Cody called me. Said your truck's already fixed. Not that you should be driving."

"I was talking to Dr. Katz about the man I shared the room with, about whether he's going to make it."

"The longer on the vent the worse the prognosis. Surprised he was in a room with you. ICU must have been packed." Caitlin pulled out onto the road. "You're lucky you didn't have to go on one."

"But he looks immaculate. Not a scratch on him. Just a little blue."

"Those are the scary ones. Fine on the outside, all the damage on the inside. I've been to see your father, you know. I didn't know how long you'd be in, so I checked on him. He thought I was his aide. I was in scrubs, of course. I didn't say anything about the accident. The nurse said he's been agitated, hallucinating, seeing little men. They're adjusting his medication."

"Little men?" Stanley glanced over his shoulder. "That's a new one. We're not that far. Maybe we should go see him."

Caitlin looked over at Stanley. "And scare him half to death. Your face. It's still bruised, a little swollen. And the sutures. Give it a little time. Why didn't you tell me how far along he'd gotten?"

"You're a nurse. You know what happens. You look tired."

She cocked her head toward the backseat. "Double shift and I picked you up some groceries. It's already been a long day. Don't thank me."

On 108 now they passed out of old Sonora into the newer part, supermarkets, drug stores, and fast food; then they started climbing into the forest. Stanley opened the window. It was warm, but he could feel the cool breeze that came with altitude.

Caitlin glanced over at him, at the folder on his lap, then back to the road. "So did they go through that with you, your aftercare instructions?"

"It's from the coroner's office. Sheriff Boyd dropped it off. I'm supposed to call."

"What is it?"

"Pictures."

"Of?"

The road narrowed as they passed the sign for Mi-Wuk, 4678 feet, Population 85, and then the Mi-Wuk Inn, a pool, fake deer around it, and further up The Mi-Wuk Café, a small log cabin with gingham curtains and a closed sign in its window.

"I appreciate you driving me," Stanley said. "It's already late. It might be dark by the time you head back down the pass. You can stay overnight—in a room if you like."

"Thanks, but I don't think Aiden would appreciate that, and it's too early to be that dark."

"He doesn't want to marry you?"

"Sure, you'll be the best man. But it's not a bad idea to have someone stay with you the first night just in case."

"In case what?"

"You didn't answer my question."

"What question?"

"You know." Caitlin glanced over at the folder.

"They're pictures, but who knows what they mean, and Sheriff Boyd's not a doctor, and I was pretty out of it."

"So, what were you doing in Bodie in the middle of the night anyway? Dr. Katz said you remember some."

"Not what you think."

"So the tree drove into you?"

"I saw deer. Heard a shot. Thought I was hit," he said, even though the blast of a rifle wasn't what he'd heard but things snapping, breaking, shattering, his head whipping back and forth, and a sudden violent jar. And how could he explain what had driven him out of bed in the first place, his nightmares, Lorna draped over his back, his fruitless search through the woods, the very place he wound up in? She'd think he was crazy—and he still loved her.

"Hmm. Hunters? In the middle of the night? Good thing you didn't say little green men. Surprised they didn't send a

shrink up. You're not sleeping again, are you? I told you insom-
niacs have a short life expectancy."

"So much for double shifts."

"It's no joke, Stanley. Whatever happened to Lorna. You
know, I liked her."

"People are always more likeable dead."

"Okay, so we didn't always get along. Look at us. You know
her house's up for sale. Ray called me. Apparently Ray and Lorna never divorced. He's still on the deed. Wants you to go to the
house and clean out what's left, stuff in her closet, I think. He
got the realtor to do the rest. Ray also said the coroner called
him, but he never told me the cause of death."

"All I have is the preliminary autopsy report."

"Why didn't you tell me?"

"It doesn't say anything. Cause of death undetermined.
How's Dell?"

"I don't know. Sorry, I should have asked. The call caught
me by surprise. I mean when was the last time I spoke to Ray?
And I can't say I exactly liked him either."

"You don't like anyone."

"Most people aren't likable."

"Then how can you be a nurse?"

"ER nurse. Motel owner. People in. People out. That's us,
right?" Caitlin rolled up her window and switched on the heat.
"I forgot how chilly it can get up here. I guess the pass will be
even worse. Creepy place."

"It's where we got caught in the hail, remember on the Sonora Pass Trail? We should have tried again."

Caitlin looked over at Stanley and then back at the road and
sighed. "Well, I don't think we would have been very good at it.
I mean we can barely stand ourselves. It's a life sentence, kids,
you know. Eighteen years at least. Eighteen years of looking at
half your genes sorting themselves out."

"You were so sick," Stanley said.

"That's what happens when something dies inside you. Anyway, you better call the coroner. Find out what those pictures

mean. If there's a genetic thing. You've heard of the human genome. Strawberry Inn's up ahead, isn't it? Let's take a break, get a drink."

Coming around a bend, they drove over a wooden bridge, crossing the Stanislaus River, a frothy raging thing from all the spring melt, and then turned into a dirt lot fronting the inn, a dilapidated two-story brown shingle with a metal roof. After walking through the small, empty restaurant with plastic table-cloths, they sat down at the bar, the back wall mirrored. A tree trunk grew up through the floor right through the bar, a real one with leaves on it.

"That's so weird. I forgot about that," Caitlin said. "A friend of mine stayed in a house like that in Tahoe with a tree growing up in it. It was full of spiders."

The bartender, a muscular guy in a plaid shirt, put down two napkins.

"I guess we shouldn't drink," Caitlin said. "Probably still have pain meds in your system."

"Cokes all around," Stanley said.

The bartender pulled two glasses and filled them with ice.

Stanley reached for his wallet. "My treat. If I have any money."

"Good thing you had that with you. Otherwise, they wouldn't even have known who you were. A John Doe until you woke up. So how do you feel?" She tapped her temple. "Seems like they sprung you too soon."

The bartender put the two glasses down. "Holler if you need anything." He went to the other end of the bar and started drying glasses.

"Body still hurts. Mild headache."

"Well, you were probably thrown around a lot, even with your seatbelt on. What did Dr. Katz give you to take for pain?"

"Codeine. But it makes me sick."

"Why didn't you ask for something else? Then again they're probably afraid to give you anything stronger. They think you're depressed. Asked me if you were."

"What'd you say?"

"Said you were crazy." Caitlin lifted her glass. "So, what are you going to do?"

Stanley, cradling his glass, peered down at the floating cubes, at the rising bubbles. "Get caught up. The motel, you know."

She put her glass down and looked at him. "About Lorna. Are you going to call the coroner or not?"

"People die and you don't know why." He repeated her line.

"Ha. Ha. Ha. If you weren't so stubborn—or afraid."

Stanley peered at himself in the mirror, at the sutures holding him together, at Caitlin beside him, her hair in a ponytail. "Okay, you're right. I couldn't sleep. I'd been having nightmares." Stanley shrugged. "It doesn't bother me Ray getting the house, you know. It'll go to Dell eventually. Right? That's what Lorna would have wanted."

"Well, I told Ray it was a bad idea you cleaning out the house under the circumstances."

Stanley drained his glass and peered down at the bottom, at the leftover ice. "I guess he's moved on already, huh?"

"Ray probably moved on long before Lorna died. He left her, right?"

"Is that what you did long before we split?" Stanley looked at her reflection and then over at the bartender stacking glasses in a pyramid now.

"Well, at least I didn't move a million miles from my kid. Illinois? Wisconsin? Or wherever he went. Some god-awful place in the Midwest." Caitlin slid off her seat. "Let's go."

Stanley dropped some money on the bar and followed her out.

Caitlin turned back on the road. "So, what do they look like, those pictures?"

"Oceans and sea creatures. Like a Rorschach test."

"Sounds like tissue samples. But what of?" Caitlin turned sharply, heading up another series of switchbacks.

"Her heart maybe. That preliminary report said something about abnormalities, but I couldn't make sense of it. Not that it matters much anymore."

"What? Are you kidding? Of course it does. What's wrong with you? If there's something wrong with her heart, there might be something wrong with yours as well. And what about Dell? What happened to her could happen to him. Can't you get Cody to stay with you for a few days? At least until you see the coroner. People who live alone, there's no one to find you, to get you help. And nowhere near a hospital."

"They helicoptered me out."

"You got lucky, that caretaker finding you. You could have easily been out there longer, froze to death if a storm came through. And then what?" She sighed. "These switchbacks are a drag. How much farther? I don't know how you do it going back and forth to see your father."

"Don't you miss it, the trees, the aspen?"

"It's pretty all right. But the cold. The long winters. It's not like Sonora doesn't have any trees."

"You're almost there. 395's coming up."

Caitlin slowed down. "Finally. A straight road."

Stanley peered out his window as the ranchland passed, the sun sinking behind it. And then the sidewalks started up and on the outskirts of town the Mobil station and then the rest of it, more gas stations and restaurants, the low-rise motels up against the surrounding mountains, and then finally in the distance his own sign, The Sleepy River Lodge, the no vacancy sign flashing red, coming into view.

"So how does it feel to be back?"

"Like I never left."

"Well, you weren't gone that long." Caitlin pulled into the lot, near the empty pool, the hose still lying there like a dead snake. He got out of the car, Caitlin following. In the office Stanley turned on the light. On the counter was a stack of mail and a note from Cody taped to the computer screen. *Closed up early. No check-ins. Fish fed. Truck's in the lot. Keys in the drawer. Welcome back, buddy.*

"You should get some rest now," Caitlin said. "The motel can wait."

"Sure you don't want to stay? You can have a river-view

room. We can look at the autopsy report and pictures." He put the folder down on the counter.

"That's tempting, but you should talk to the coroner first. I'm just a nurse. I'll be fine. You're the damaged one. What's wrong with civilization anyway? Why couldn't you have just stayed in Sonora?"

"This is civilization. God's country."

She laughed. "An atheist in God's country."

"Agnostic."

"Right. Anyway, if you start feeling bad, nauseous or your headache gets worse call 911. Hopefully your heart won't stop. Goodnight." The door shut, he was alone. He read Cody's note again. He wasn't like the young people who left town soon as they could. City life, Stanley had told them, wasn't any less alienating than alpine life, but the colorful facade of LA or San Francisco was too tempting. Coming back into town tonight Stanley understood why. He saw just how small Bridgeport really was.

He stepped into his unit. His vague notions of Caitlin staying, of trying again, had dissolved into the fuzziness he now felt. His fish were still alive though, swimming back and forth. It seemed he should unpack, but there wasn't anything to unpack since his clothes, cut off at the hospital, had been tossed, Caitlin buying him new ones. Sitting at his kitchen counter, he opened the folder and peered at the churning ocean, the salty brew again, as if it were shot from space, and thought of his roommate, the man he'd left behind, the sound of the air forced down his throat. *You could be in danger. What happened to her could happen to you.* Sheriff Boyd's and Caitlin's voices came back to him. He looked around the room, at his couch, TV, at the back window, at the slice of purple-blue light between the drawn curtains. He felt his heart start to pound, echoing in his ears. He went back out to the check-in counter, tried to focus on an object—the deer mounted on the wall, glassy brown eyes looking down at him—but still his eyes kept roaming, landing on the window facing 395. It was as if he expected the culprit to be staring back at him—the rifle-toting hunter he'd made up, the taunting drunk Rusty, the shadow looming over his terror-stricken sister. He'd weathered such anxiety before, the attacks starting after Lorna's death—and the nightmares. Her body, her hair flung forward, the white of her neck; the funeral home wouldn't let him see her. The dead never look like themselves and you wouldn't want to remember her that way and crap like that they'd told him. Once, when they'd been kids, someone kept calling their house in the middle of the night, saying, "You're going to die tonight." His mother, hysterical, refused to sleep. A trace had been put on their line, but Stanley knew it was a prank, some kid opening the white pages, randomly picking a name, finding a willing victim. And so he'd calmed himself, and, taking a deep breath, he felt his heart settle into rhythm, his muscles relax, and he walked back into his unit, into the bathroom and splashed water on his face. He watched it swirl down the drain, then looked back up at his dripping face, the first time he'd really studied the aftermath up close, the suture tracks running haphazardly, the left side bruised, eye still purple, cheek a sickly yellowish-green. "Not half bad considering," Caitlin had said at his hospital bedside, accessing the damage in the bright light of day after he'd come to. "These sorts of injuries heal," she'd said, being kind. He patted his face dry with a towel, then smiled at himself in the mirror. No pain, but his face felt tight. As he shut the cabinet and turned away, he heard the motel bell ring. He walked out of the living room into the office. Had Caitlin changed her mind? A last-minute check-in? Stanley opened the door.

"Heard they sprung you today," Sheriff Boyd said. "Aren't you going to let me in?"

Stanley backed away. "There's no coffee."

The sheriff waved his hand. "Looks better, your face. Less swollen. You're just lucky you didn't kill yourself. Those pictures I left. You looked at them?"

"I just got back."

A voice came crackling over the sheriff's radio. He listened to it and then turned to Stanley. "I don't know what happened in Bodie. But I don't believe trees run into people. Accidents happen, sure. There's a reason parks close after sundown. I won't pretend to understand—I didn't know Lorna—but there are people out there who lose people and go to their grave never knowing what happened. The body never found, no one gets punished." The radio came back on. A voice crackled through again, the words all broken up.

They were getting a late start, the tour outfit waiting on an updated weather report, and when the confirmation call had come in Grace picked up the phone right away. Then, slipping out of the room, Elwood sleeping through all of it, she headed to the lot near the check-in building where she saw a small group of people gathered near a purple van with large tinted windows, *Desert Adventures* stenciled on its door. A tall man in white pants and a navy windbreaker, breaking away from the group, trotted over to her and extended his hand. "Grace, right? Bram, your tour guide." He had gray-blue eyes, a shock of straight blondish-brown hair, and a handsome tanned, lined face. Clipboard in hand, he reminded her of an aging camp counselor or a sun-weathered sailor. "Okay, everyone, here's our holdout— Grace." In a circle everyone started shaking hands, crisscrossing arms in a comical fashion on the brink of their expedition, eight of them—besides herself and Bram, a grandfather, his three teenage grandsons in shorts and Death Valley T-shirts, and a woman in culottes, a purse slung over her shoulder, who kept saying, "I hope it isn't too bumpy," and her teenage son, a large ungainly boy in baggy shorts with pale, pimply skin and a mop of brown curly hair nearly covering half his face. Then, through the van's back doors, they loaded up, the grandsons scrambling ahead of everybody, taking the first row, Grace in a middle row, and the mother and her son in the back row across the aisle from each other. The grandfather, easily carsick, sat up front beside Bram. A few seats were empty. No one, as far as Grace could tell, noticed that she was the only one alone.

"Okay, here we go," Bram said, shutting his door, "full speed ahead. Everybody buckled up? Weather report says a cold front's coming in, possible storm in the high desert, but I assured the powers at large that no act of nature could stop this group."

The three grandsons, looking at each other, laughed, and from behind her Grace heard the mother giggle, saying, "Oh dear, what have we gotten ourselves into, Pete?"

"But just in case. Satellite phone." Bram lifted it off the dashboard. "Your life is taken seriously here at Desert Adventures. Not to worry." Engine started, he pulled out of the lot. As they passed the gas station, Grace peered at its pumps, a camper alongside one, and behind it, the garage, door rolled up. Their own car battery replaced yesterday, she and Elwood had ended up driving out to the Ubehebe Crater afterward, Elwood getting what he wanted—his wildflower pictures on an unusually windless day—and so she didn't see why he'd want to go back, the crater the first scheduled stop on the tour. Waking him this morning, it would have only ended in a fight, even though they never really fought, just disagreed until the disagreement eventually drifted off. Instead she'd left a note—*On the tour. Back before dark. Don't worry*—on her pillow. Grace peered out her window, the van having passed the golf course and the ranger station.

"There's Mustard Canyon," Bram shouted. "Off to the left. See those old wagons? Mule teams pulled them, carrying borax."

"Borax? What's that?" one of the grandsons asked.

"Your dog's name," one of the others said, laughing.

"Soap," Bram said. "To wash your clothes. Big money in its day."

Twenty minutes later they came to a large field of low-growing brush in oddly uniform rows as if they'd been planted that way. "That, my friends, is Devil's Cornfield. One of the eeriest places you'll ever see, except for the Racetrack Playa, of course. *Pluchea Sericea* or arrowweed. That's what the Indians called it because they used the shoots to make arrows. Soil and sand form the mounds the plant grows from."

"Looks like heads," one of the grandsons said.

"With their hair standing on end," another grandson said.

"Okay," Bram said, "here's our turn off, the road out to the Ubehebe Crater, first stop on the itinerary." Then Bram began to prattle about alluvial fans, Death Valley folklore, Death Valley Scotty, buried above the Inn, a charlatan who'd talked himself into a cozy friendship with a wealthy insurance magnate, living his days out in the magnate's castle known now as Scotty's Castle, tours available, and various plants—holly, mesquite, Mormon tea, and the parasitic golden thread—all, Grace assumed, from a pre-set script. Then, approaching an orange roadwork sign and a line of stopped cars, Bram pulled off to the side of the road and said, "Good opportunity to stretch our legs and take a look at some *Larea tridentata*, creosote bush. A whole field of them out there." He opened the back doors, and they unloaded, encircling one of the bushes, small, green, waxy-looking leaves blooming tiny yellow flowers. Bram pulled off a leaf. "Go ahead," he said, "rub it between your fingers. Put it to your nose." And when Grace did, she recoiled, the chemical smell nearly making her swoon.

"Smells like gasoline," the grandfather said. "Who would have guessed?"

"Ooh. I'm going to vomit," one of the grandsons said, and the other two jumped away from him.

"Enough now," the grandfather said.

Leaning toward Grace, the woman in the culottes said, "I don't think I've ever seen this kind of bush. Why's it smell so bad?"

"Bitter," Bram said. "That's why we swallow pills. But put a few leaves in a tea and away what ails you goes—flu, sinusitis, infections, even athlete's foot."

The grandsons, pinching their noses, started laughing and pushing each other, saying, "Yeah, you need that. Your stinky feet."

"Good for shrinking kidney and gall stones too," Bram continued. "But take too much and it's toxic. Jackrabbit is the only animal that'll eat it when it can't get something better." Bram looked over at the road. "Okay, let's load up."

As they continued, the road started to slope up, running through vast, colorful rock beds, plants and cacti sprouting from them, flanking the distant mountains. Besides other cars on the road and the construction behind them, there was nothing else, no gas stations or restaurants. Just the mountains and the rocks and their van speeding through it, and Grace, alone among strangers, as they moved closer to the crater—really a series of craters, one large one, which Grace and Elwood had hiked around yesterday, and a few smaller ones.

Bram slowed down as they approached the ranger booth. "Just got to pay the toll," he said as he pulled up alongside the booth, even though Grace knew it was unmanned or at least was yesterday and the year before when she and Elwood had first gone out there on their own. "Guess Ranger Joe's sleeping late. That's where they live, over there to the right, in those wooden barracks. And over here, to the left, is the last bathroom you'll see for a long time." He pulled up to a wooden one-story building, its front door padlocked, a pay phone in front of it, open desert behind it, where wind was already kicking up sand into dust devils. "See those doors over to the side there? They're open. Last chance or forever hold your bladder." He turned off the engine, trotted behind the van, and opened the back doors.

After Grace got out, the wind, gusting, pushed her sideways, and she had to put her hand against the van to right herself. Then she zipped her jacket and started walking toward the building.

"Gosh," the woman said, walking beside Grace, "I guess we should have brought coats. I didn't know it would be so cold here. It's cold here, isn't it, Pete?" She turned around, but there was no one there. "Oh, I guess he's already in the restroom."

Grace glanced down at her watch, thinking Elwood was probably shaving now or eating a late breakfast at the 49er, at the counter watching the chefs in the big hats scramble eggs, the whole place smelling of bacon. Or maybe he was roombound, note in hand, stewing. She glanced over her shoulder at the payphone, its coiled wire dangling, receiver missing, and then followed the woman into the restroom. From the next stall over, the woman said loudly, "In Modesto, we have to keep the heaters running all winter to keep our cacti alive. We have a koi pond too, fenced off 'cause of the raccoons. You have raccoons where you live? Ours don't even really eat the fish, just bite their heads off and leave them for dead. Who ever heard of animals killing things they don't eat?"

Grace, out of the stall now, washed her hands at the lone sink, and then pushed the rusty dryer button. As she held her hands under the hot air, the woman, out of the stall now, started washing her hands. "Lagmore's our last name," she shouted over the loud whirl, "and the name of our shop. Harry, my husband, he's the real expert. But he's dead, last spring, and truth is I don't really know much about cacti. I mean I didn't even know the desert could get cold in spring." The dryer, silent now, the woman, hands dripping, sent it whirling again and kept talking. "Emphysema. Couldn't take a step without gasping. Wasn't really living. I mean what is living? And your husband, did he pass too? Is that why you're alone? I noticed your rings. I still wear mine." Grace and the woman walked out of the restroom. "Well, I still have Pete. Not much of a talker, though. You know how they are—teenagers. Or maybe it's the sadness that never goes away, him losing his father. This trip, I thought, might be good for him. He likes to take pictures. The moving rocks. But Pete's not like other boys, and now with no father even less like other boys. And I'm a woman. Oh my gosh, this wind. Where is everybody?"

The back doors open, Grace stepped up into the van, the woman following, lodging herself back in the corner.

Grace turned to the woman. "My husband's back at the hotel. He didn't want to go."

The woman looked out her window. "Oh, there they are. Filing back in like soldiers." She turned back to Grace. "You know, I worry. My son…he won't tell me, but I think the kids—they bully him. Good thing it's his senior year."

Everyone seated, Bram started the van again. "Okay, folks. I know the Ubehebe's first up, but I think given the wind and the front coming in we should head directly to the Racetrack just in case things go bad. Get in. Get out."

Elwood had warned her about this when she'd first brought up the tour a week or so before they'd left on the trip, the bad weather, how these tours were usually rushed, but she wasn't bothered; thus far it was everything she'd thought it was going to be, and now despite the bad weather, she felt at ease, having left everything behind. Bram, turning left onto a narrow road, passed the turn-off for the crater's parking lot and brought the van to a stop where the pavement ended and the washboard began. The grandsons, cameras in hand, were out of their seatbelts and pushing each other out of the way trying to get a picture out their window of the street sign, Racetrack Road. The van idling, Grace tried to get a better look at the road, the worst washboard she'd ever seen, pitted and rocky, too narrow for a passing car, and serpentine, winding downward, framed by rocky berms, those sharp lava rocks the woman from the en clave said ate tires. But what bewildered her most was that she didn't remember the road, a road she and Elwood had traveled that first year out in a jeep with the rangers, Jared's old purple Cougar the only thing she did remember, parked at the curve of the playa, window halfway down, as if it had driven itself out to some deserted drive-in movie lost in time.

"Okay, boys," Bram said, "back in your seats now. Seatbelts on. Now take a good look behind you. It's the last piece of pavement you'll see for a long time. Fifty-two miles roundtrip to be specific, so if you're going to bail…" He looked in his rearview mirror and then nodded his head. "Okay. Good. Just as I thought. Now listen. Whatever you do don't lean forward, don't rest your head against the window, and don't take your seatbelt off. No talking either. It's not possible. Human beings can't. Not on terrain like this. Here we go." Dropping off the paved road, the van began rattling immediately. Bram picked up speed. A slow approach always made the rattling worse. A certain amount of recklessness was necessary, Grace knew, from the tamer washboard roads she and Elwood had driven to tourist sites; and as the van started vibrating violently, falling into and lurching out of holes, its tires skimming close to the berm, Grace tried to focus on what was out her window. She'd brought pad and pen, fearing memory might outwit her again, even brought a camera, a cheap drug-store one, something she never carried, though at home she kept an obligatory photo album. She pulled the camera out and tried holding it up to her eye, but she couldn't steady her hand, the rattling so violent the skin on her face vibrated, and, when the van plunged into a hole again and lurched back out, her kidneys seemed to leap up then settle back down. At any minute she feared the whole outer shell of the van itself might slip off, and suddenly, strapped in their seats, they'd be exposed, just the skeleton of the van left. She dropped the camera back in her bag and braced herself.

"Oh my," Grace heard the woman call out, her voice quivering.

Grace glanced back at her—she was pressed against the wall, clutching her purse—and then directly behind her, at the woman's son who seemed to have nodded off, head drooping, body pitched forward, rocking back and forth as if praying, only his seatbelt keeping him from tumbling into her seat.

"Check it out," Bram said. "Joshuas. Off to the left. Look at them. Aren't they crazy? People. Just like us."

"Hey, I thought we weren't supposed to talk," one of the grandsons said, and Bram, laughing, said, "You. Not me," while Grace looked at the trees, growing upslope toward the mouth of the mountains, larger and more numerous than the ones she and Elwood had seen in the Panamints on their way in. Surely they'd been there her first time out, she thought. Grace felt the van slow down, up ahead an intersection, a weathered wooden signpost: TEA KETTLE JUNCTION. Sitting atop it were two tea kettles—one tarnished silver, the other red and chipped—and hanging from the sign itself were lots of other kettles jumbled together, clanking in the wind. "We'll take a little break here for pictures," Bram said, turning off the engine. He jogged around back and opened the doors, letting cold air in. The grandsons scrambled out first, then the woman's son, then the woman, and finally Grace, slipping on her jacket. It was cold, and though the sky was still blue, gray-bellied clouds were breaking away from the mountaintops. Grace looked back down the road, wondering how many miles they'd come, wondering what good a satellite phone would do in a flash flood, water being far faster than cars. But here at the Tea Kettle Junction sign everyone was snapping pictures of each other while Bram, leaning against the van, clicked his tongue and said, "Can't believe not a one of you brought a kettle. Your chance to leave your mark."

"Don't you want to have a picture?" the woman said, coming up to Grace. "Pete can take one of us beside the kettles, and I can send it to you. Pete?" she called over to him—he was off a ways near the berm, nudging a rock with his foot. "Can you come over here and take a picture of us, please?" She lifted her hand to her brow as if she were having trouble seeing him, and then she turned to Grace. "He doesn't like taking pictures of people. Just things. Animals and things."

"That's okay," Grace said. "My husband's like that too. He's all flowers."

"Okay. Back in! Away we go!" Bram shouted. He pointed toward the sky. "Storm's coming in."

Back in the van again, they continued up the road, gradually gaining elevation. Bram driving fast, only slowing down when an occasional car, usually a jeep, a rental—*Carl's Desert Jeeps* printed on the side—came from the other direction and he needed to let it pass and all the people inside smiled and waved. It was a tight squeeze, one car having to heave up onto the berm to let the other pass.

"Grandstand's next. Then north end of the playa," Bram shouted. As the van continued rattling along, climbing up, Grace could see down below part of the playa—vast, beige, and perfectly flat-looking. Bram brought the van to a stop near a strange outcropping of large, smooth oval-shaped rocks piled atop one another in a tall heap like something from a tropical island heaved up in a tsunami. This, too, she had no recollection of. "The Grandstand at last. Bring your jackets, folks. It's only going to get colder," he said, opening the back door, even though no one had brought one on the trip but her. Outside Grace looked up, the gray clouds, more plentiful now, starting to merge, one covering the sun. Shivering, she zipped her jacket. Everyone walked quickly toward the jumbled rocks, the grandsons well ahead, hands stuffed in their pockets, shoulders bunched up. Grace, the woman, and her son followed. Bram and the grandfather came up the rear. At the base, everyone watched the grandsons scramble up. At the top they all shouted, "Hey," waving their arms as if they were lost or shipwrecked on a South Seas island. But of course there were no waves lapping at a shoreline, no animal life, except for a crow soaring above, cawing.

"No horsing around up there, boys," Bram called up to them. "Storm's on the way. Come on down."

"Ah, not already," the boys called down. "We just got here."

"You're to listen to Bram, boys," the grandfather shouted up. "If it starts raining those rocks are going to get slick."

"Look how steep that is, Pete," the woman said, as the grandsons started picking their way down. "Don't you want to take a picture of it, these strange rocks?"

But the boy just kept watching the grandsons descend.

After they loaded up again, the road started pitching steeply downward, and Grace, bracing herself, hung on, the rest of the playa now coming into sight.

"Just a little longer," Bram shouted. "Lunch will be served. Water and granola bars. Nothing too heavy. The trip back—" A gust of wind cut him off, and the van pulled sideways. "Nothing to worry about," he shouted, righting the van. He slowed down as the van rounded a corner. "And there they are, the mysterious ladies. The moving rocks of the Racetrack Playa. What you came for, awaiting you."

As they kept descending, Grace peered at the rocks scattered randomly across the playa, all different sizes, not smooth or oval like the Grandstand's but rough-edged, their tails, which Grace could see even from here, evidence of their travels, imprinted behind them. Bram turned off the engine. No other cars were around, just them and their van, and Grace trying to remember exactly where Jared's car had been parked, his purple Cougar, among the vast emptiness.

"Come on. Hurry. Let's go," Grace heard the grandsons saying as they unloaded, and everyone scattered, each finding a rock, squatting down or taking pictures of it. Only Bram had stayed behind in the van, sitting in the driver's seat, his door open a little, out of the wind, which was stronger now, gusting every once in a while. Grace, by herself at the perimeter, marveled at the weathered floor beneath her feet, not smooth at all as it had appeared earlier but brittle and cracked into an endless pattern of octagons. She glanced down at her bag hanging from her shoulder, in it her camera, but taking pictures was the last thing she wanted to do now, the camera, she now realized, just an excuse, her way of persuading Elwood or herself that there really was good reason to return. "Well, you have your memories," was what most well-wishers imposed on her, but she didn't believe in a still life, a static picture. Nor did she believe in erasing memory, no matter how bad, though at the same time she understood why someone might try. A man from the grief therapy group, having found his daughter hanging in the backyard, had chopped the tree down, and when that didn't work, he tried hypnosis, a therapist peeling his memory back to that morning—her out the front door, backpack on, off to school. *Bye, Dad.* But then the man couldn't remember if he'd said he'd loved her that morning. Grace turned away from the rocks, looking back at the road at the place where it curved. Was that where Jared's car had been parked? No blood. No footprints. No shred of clothes or hair. No evidence of struggle. No autopsy photo. Just a boy who'd managed to get his car twenty-six miles down a jagged road unscathed and maybe ambled off or got sucked into the sky Castaneda-style. She moved her gaze to the surrounding rocky outcroppings where she assumed the rocks or "the ladies," as Bram and the scientists called them, breaking free, ended up on the playa, sent tumbling by storm winds. After that, sleet and more wind gave them legs. Rita, Adele, Louise, Maryann—they'd all been named by scientists, but Grace could hardly remember who was who. The book she'd gotten about the place listed so many, their profiles—height, weight, shape—as well as some of their quirks, as if it were a beauty pageant. Grace stepped gingerly onto the playa, fearing her own weight might make the surface somehow crumble, changing the pattern, but the surface was not as brittle or fragile as she'd thought. She stopped at one rock, studying its trajectory, its tail, this one a straight shooter; others, she noticed as she scanned the playa, looped inexplicably, leaving a shallow imprint with their own set of berms. Her fellow travelers, lightly dressed, gathered around them, the lore of the place making them immune to the cold wind blowing through, the sky now a solid gray ceiling. For her, though, the rocks held no mystery—the scientists, despite never seeing the rocks move, figured it out—just as the question of why Jared had made a solo trip out here didn't seem as puzzling now. And maybe her fellow travelers didn't know or care to know the rational explanation for how the rocks moved. It was the not knowing that spurred people on, perpetuating the mystery, and who, Grace thought, was she to ruin that, in this case a bit of fun? Grace touched her cheek. Except for freak storms, rain in the desert at sea level usually evaporated before it hit the ground, but here at altitude, real rain and sleet were possible; despite Elwood's warning and her own concerns, she wouldn't have minded getting stuck in a storm at least for a while, thinking maybe this time the rocks might reveal themselves, letting her see what no one had ever seen, the playa transforming itself into a moving floor, a ballroom of waltzing women in a cold, raging storm. This was what fascinated her—not that the rocks moved but that they did so in their own good time, without audience or fanfare. And maybe this is what had drawn Jared out, why he'd come alone when his friends had stayed behind at the Ranch, at the pool, girl-watching, as they'd said. Grace felt a raindrop hit her cheek, and a gust of wind blew through. She touched her face again and felt the rain on her fingertips. Others had their own theories of course—the rangers with their statistics about young men Jared's age, risk-takers, wandering off, unable to find their way back. These were the ones who usually went out too far with too little water into the Mesquite Sand Dunes and died. Or maybe, like the Castaneda woman who'd walked off into the desert, Jared had been disillusioned. Or gay—another ranger theory—and didn't want to find his way back. Or maybe, walking off by his own volition, he was living as a brand-new person, a brand-new life, perfectly content.

"All right. Time's up!" Grace heard Bram shouting. Out of the van now, he was waving them in, but no one was moving. He took a few steps onto the playa and put his hands on his hips. "Come on now, folks. Rain's coming. Think flash floods. Think last chance!" He kept waving his arms, and finally everyone began trudging toward the van, the rain coming down steadily now, drops beading and bursting on the playa's surface. Grace, back first, stepped up into the van, where Bram, now holding the doors open, was still shouting, "Come on! Let's beat the storm before it beats us."

Seated inside now, Grace watched the group straggle in, the grandsons filing past her, their hair damp; up front the grandfather got himself in the passenger seat. Then from behind her, Grace heard the woman say, "Where's Pete?"

Grace looked out to the playa, but the rain, coming down steadily now, was graying everything, and all she could see was the outline of Bram in the distance out on the playa, bent forward slightly, and she could hear him yelling, "Pete! Come on! Where are you? Pete!" while the woman, who'd moved over to Grace's side of the van, pressed her face against the window. "Now where do you think he's gone to?" she said, her voice wavering a little. "Those rocks. You wouldn't know it, but that's all he talked about before the trip, how they move. And now with the rain he probably thinks he's going to see them move. I better go out there."

"I don't think that's a good idea," Grace said. "You don't even have a coat."

"What about yours?" the woman said, starting to stand upright now.

"It's raining harder now. You might lose your way."

The woman leaned forward, pressing her face to the window again. "Wait. Is that them out there?"

Grace saw two figures, one tall, one shorter, taking form in the gray.

The woman went back to her seat. "How about you? You have any kids?"

"A son."

The back doors opened, a blast of cold air rushing in, and everybody turned around as the boy climbed in, camera in hand, T-shirt soaked, hair hanging down, dripping.

"For heaven's sake," the woman said, "didn't you hear Bram calling? You want to ruin that camera? Get us trapped here? And everyone waiting for you."

The boy sat down in his seat and looked at his mother and then down at his camera.

Grace put on her seatbelt.

Bram, in the front now, started the engine. "All right. All accounted for. Nothing to worry about, folks, now that we're underway. Just a little rain and a short delay. Remember we have the satellite phone."

The van started moving. Everyone was quiet, only the sound of the windshield wipers whipping back and forth and the crunch of rock beneath the tires. Grace glanced over her shoulder. Both the woman and the son, turned away from each other now, were looking out their windows. In front of her the grandsons, their dark hair shiny from the rain, sat upright, looking straight ahead, no one annoyed, it seemed to her, that they couldn't stay longer. Rather they seemed quietly exhilarated, having hauled out to a place few people would ever see. Heat on, windows fogged up and rain stained, the van started to climb back up to the Grandstand, vibrating, lurching, jostling Grace around, but now for some reason she didn't mind it as much. As brutal as it had been on the way in, the rough road now comforted her, and she hung on happily, one hand grasping the seat belt that crossed her chest, the other braced against the van wall. In this position she felt perfectly safe. She glanced over her shoulder at the boy. Head drooping, hair swinging, camera slung around his neck, he'd slipped back into his desert narcolepsy. She turned around, peering at the back of the grandsons' bobbing heads, and then out her window back at Tea Kettle Junction. The various kettles, which had seemed so colorful on the way in, now seemed dull in the gray rain, more like junk than whimsical art, the desert sharpening and blurring everything. Then they came to the Joshuas. Though hard to see from her side of the van, she imagined them pitched up on the broad slope, grateful for the rain, but maybe cold or a little lonely as their warm van warily made its way along the pitted road, rattling terribly, leaving them behind.

"Look," Bram said, glancing in his rearview mirror, "I was just kidding. Permission to speak. And don't worry. I expect we'll get out of this just fine. See?" He lifted the phone again and quickly put it back down, grabbing the wheel, as the van lurched sharply to one side.

But Grace, in no rush to get back to the manicured lawns and date fields of Furnace Creek, wasn't thinking of rescue. It had become painfully clear from her time in the grief therapy group how little parents, pinned down by guilt and denial, understood the various pulls on their children or themselves. Here, in the stormy backcountry though, where Jared had disappeared, she somehow felt protected and began to understand why people climbed vertical rock, jumped from airplanes, how easy it was to be pulled out, around just one more corner, how it was nobody's fault. She looked at her watch, then back out the window, tall mountains in view now, just the dark fuzzy outlines of them hovering in the distance. She knew this meant they were approaching the end of the road, that Bram wouldn't need to use the satellite phone, call in a May Day. She looked back over at the woman again still up against the window and then over at the boy, upright now, eyes open, hair wet but no longer dripping, hands cradling his camera. It occurred to her then that he hadn't said a word the entire trip. *Did you get any good pictures?* Grace wanted to ask, but the van shifted right suddenly, and she turned around quickly, bracing herself against the wall.

"Look at that. Civilization in sight. Pavement awaits us. If the wind doesn't get us first," Bram said, laughing.

Grace felt the van lift up over the lip, and suddenly the rattling stopped, and everyone started clapping.

The van idling, Bram turned in his seat, trying to bow a little. "At Desert Adventures our passengers' safety is paramount. However, we're not quite home yet."

"I'm hungry," one of the grandsons said.

"Lunch is served. Bon appétit," Bram said, tossing granola bars over his shoulder while the grandsons, laughing, tried to catch them and pass them back.

As the van started moving again, Grace turned around, this time looking past the boy, out the back windows to Racetrack Road, which shone oddly white now through the gray, almost glittering, as if the rain had washed it clean, smoothing it out, as it spiraled downward, receding into gray. She suddenly felt the urge to jump up and shout, *Wait! Stop!*, beating her fists against the back window as if she'd left something behind. It was all she could do to keep herself still. She looked around. Surely someone must have noticed her distress, but everyone was eating. And what would they think had she actually gotten up and beat the glass? Irrational passenger, woman gone mad? Hallucinating? Bram would need to use his satellite phone after all. Afterward, she would need to see *someone*—a therapist or such—as Elwood had wanted her to do, as many of the parents in the grief therapy group did as if the grieving were being quietly instructed to have an affair, the question *who are you seeing* often whispered around the room between sips of coffee after a meeting broke up. To her, such post-meeting gossip seemed amusingly salacious, though it turned out that her own refusal to see someone had made her the most scandalous, spurring even more incessant whispering. Of course Elwood had been as chaste as her, not having seen anyone, but it was the women that were most expected to go, to perpetually revisit their trauma and then discuss their sessions with other women in vague, useless terms: "Yes, it's been helpful." "I've only been to a few sessions." "By all means, I'll give you his number." Therapist or psychic—she didn't think it mattered.

Bram brought the van to a stop again at the entrance to the Ubehebe Crater. A gust of wind came through, rocking the van. Turning in his seat, he looked back at everyone. "Now listen, I know it's on the itinerary, but it's late, and the wind is going to be ferocious up there. You'll freeze to death too. No jackets and all. We'll be lucky the wind doesn't tear off the doors. And if we even make it to the edge, you might be blown over and killed. Then you'll never get any decent pictures."

"Isn't that what postcards are for?" A voice came from the very back of the van, surprisingly deep, perfectly modulated with a subtle rise at the end that sounded to Grace like polite sarcasm.

"Pete!" the mother said, sitting upright now.

"And I'm a surgeon." A faint voice came from the front. Everyone turned toward the grandfather. "If you're dead, I can bring you back to life."

The grandsons looked at each other, smiling. "Go, Grandpa!" one of them said.

"You have the satellite phone." The boy spoke again.

The mother, smiling, clapped her hands together. "That's right, Pete, in case we need rescue."

Bram shook his head. "Seriously now, folks. I'm responsible for you."

"We'll sign a waiver," one of the grandsons said. "Isn't that what they're called, Grandpa, in case you kill someone?"

"Or get killed," Bram said.

"Well, maybe it's not such a good idea," the grandfather said. "Your mother—"

"Oh, come on, Grandpa," they all said. "When are we ever going to come back here? It's our only chance."

"Grace?" Bram said. "Aren't you going to say anything?"

She knew it was crazy, getting out of the van under these conditions; plus she was just here yesterday. And she would have been angry if Jared had done something so dangerous, but as she looked at the grandsons' expectant faces, the wipers up front going back and forth, their snug van idling at the base of the road up to the crater, she shrugged. "If we go quickly…" she said, and everybody started clapping.

"Well then, brave ones. At your command." He drove up a short, steep hill into a small parking lot right below the rim, pulling into a spot when another gust rocked the van, making it creak. "I told you," Bram said, "this will make *The Wizard of Oz* look like a minor storm. A warmer, dryer Furnace Creek awaits you if you'd only let me take you there. Sure you want to do this?" He looked in the rearview mirror and then turned off the engine. "Okay. Five minutes tops." He zipped up his jacket and pulled up his hood and tightened it. Grace wiped the fog from her window trying to get a better look up at the rim, but it all seemed gray, sky and rim merging. Well, at least they were on high ground, weren't they? The wind here was the real danger. When it lulled, Bram jumped out, slamming his door shut, and ran around the back. Out her window he was a quick-moving blur. She felt a blast of cold air blow in again as the doors opened, and she got to her feet.

"Okay," Bram shouted, "remember five minutes and we're out."

Grace put her hood up, tying it tight, then followed the woman and her son out. Outside the wind whipped at her, pushing her sideways. Recovering, she braced her back against the van and dropped her head as the grandsons unloaded. She looked up at the rim again, but everything was gray as if the earth had rotated, turning turbulent, a witch's brew, and she wondered if she'd made a mistake. Hanging together they all trudged up the embankment, up a black gravel slope of crushed volcanic rock, feet sinking into it, the wind, a giant hand, pushing them forward, never really stopping, lifting the gravel, mixing it with rain. Yesterday, though, with Elwood it had been serene, ethereal, white scrub rising from black volcanic rock like small ghosts, the crater floor, some 400 feet down, a sandy, rusted-colored circle, a few creosote bushes, encircled by dark walls. Looking over at her fellow travelers now inching toward the rim, the wind still blowing, swirling, shifting directions, Grace suddenly stopped, panicked again just as she had been when they'd crossed the threshold from Racetrack Road to pavement, wanting to cry out *Wait! Stop! Turn around!* But they were all bent over, hair flying as they neared the edge, and, wind howling, she wasn't sure anyone would even hear her and so she kept moving. At the rim now, it was hard to tell where the edge was. The rain was stinging her eyes, and her jacket was soaked through. Shivering, she tried to brace her legs, but the wind made her feel weightless. It could lift her, carrying her like a kite, pinning her until it lulled, sending her plummeting to the crater bottom. But somehow they'd arranged themselves in a line, standing side by side, arms hooked into one another's, forming a human chain, the cold hand of the wind still behind them, inching them closer to the edge. Then Bram, his jacket billowing, broke from the chain, and waved his arms over his head, shouting, "Step back!" But another gust came through, knocking the grandfather forward. The grandsons, grabbing him, pulled him back from the edge while everyone else dropped hands, and turned around, starting back. But it wasn't easy, going downslope, fighting wind, the visibility poor. Grace felt her feet sinking into the wet gravel. "Keep moving!" she heard Bram shout, but she couldn't see where he was, in front or behind her, and she stumbled, falling back. On the ground, she brushed off her hands and got back up to her feet. She looked around for the others and spotted the boy and his mother not far behind, their arms locked, stooped over, moving forward. Off to the left, two of the grandsons were propping up their grandfather, walking him forward while the third, Grace assumed, trailed somewhere behind. Grace started moving again, and she saw in the distance the outline of the van, and then she felt solid ground beneath her feet. Back in the lot now, she saw Bram waving them in once again.

In the van, Grace pulled off her hood, and everyone followed behind, dripping and breathing heavily, except the grandfather who'd been put in the front. She was dripping too, her shoes soggy, full of pebbles, the back of her pants damp. As she looked at her palms, at the scrapes, tiny bubbles of blood along the ridges, she thought of the dogcatcher's scarred hands, the panting dogs. Then she heard the back doors slam shut, and in front of her the grandsons were laughing again, shaking their heads like wet dogs. Behind her the woman was wiping her face with a tissue. Her cheeks were flushed. "Gee, that was something, wasn't it, Pete? Didn't I tell you it would be fun?"

From behind her Grace heard the snap of a camera and saw the boy aiming it at his mother, his mouth curled up into what seemed to be a smile.

"Oh, so now you take a picture." The mother chuckled.

Bram, starting the van, looked in the rearview mirror. "Everyone all right?" He looked over at the grandfather. "Doc, all right? Seatbelts on. Full steam ahead." He turned the van around and inched down the hill. Grace snapped hers on. Back on the main road now, its yellow lines seeming terribly straight, impossibly smooth after the fifty-two miles of washboard and the Ubehebe tempest, they passed through the unmanned ranger booth and then by the restroom with the broken pay phone. Everyone was quiet again, even Bram. Given the poor visibility, there was little for him to point out or maybe he was just tired or had run out of copy, his day nearly over. Grace took off her jacket and laid it on the seat next to her to dry. Out her window she couldn't even make out the distant mountains. She looked down at her watch. Though their time on the playa and the crater had been short, they were still somehow running late. Elwood would be worried, thinking they'd gotten a flat or got caught in a flash flood, but all that seemed as distant as the passing mountains, and now that it was safe, her head resting against the window, she closed her eyes and found herself on a dark street hiding behind a bush only steps from her front door. She'd had the dream before, the feeling that something was lurking, waiting for her to show herself, and when she felt the van turning, she opened her eyes, surprised to see clear sky.

"Fifteen minutes and home sweet home, folks," Bram said. "Mission accomplished. Actually, mission *fini*. Company's canceling the tour. Not enough interest. You're the last of your kind."

After everyone said their goodbyes and Bram drove off, Grace walked briskly across the parking lot to the grassy area. It was rude, running off, leaving the woman and her son behind, but Elwood would be waiting, and tomorrow would be their last full day in the park. But the woman, coming up behind Grace now, breathing heavily, said, "I meant to ask you. I never found out where you were from."

"Up north. The Bay Area."

"San Francisco? I love San Francisco. Don't we, Pete?" She turned to him. He was a few steps behind her. "The fog. The skyscrapers. Where was it you took those pictures, Pete?"

"I'm in the East Bay. El Cerrito," Grace said.

"Well, that's not that far from us, is it?" The woman opened her purse and pulled out a card. "Modesto is where we're from. On the way to Yosemite. If you ever come our way, we could have lunch and you could see our cacti."

Grace, halfway across the grassy area, looked down at the shiny card, a purple and green cactus on it, the word Lagmore's curling around it, and a phone number.

"Isn't that right, Pete?" the woman said. She patted him on the shoulder. "Going to be a senior next year then leave me too. Sacramento State. Photography, of course. Who would have thought I'd produce an artist?" The woman rubbed her arms. "A little chilly here too. Now that was a wild place. The wind. I thought it was going to blow us over. Who would have thought? What an adventure. Too bad they're canceling the tour. Just think only a few hours ago we were in the middle of nowhere. Rocks and us. I bet they like it out there, the quiet, even if it's a little lonely sometimes. Of course rocks don't need to eat, do they? Maybe it's better being a rock than a person. What do you think, Pete?"

"Sometimes people go out there and move the rocks themselves," the boy said.

"You mean the whole thing's a hoax?" the woman said. "Or maybe both's true—the rocks move themselves and people move them too. Oh, look how crowded the pool is. I hear it's a hot spring pool, stays the same temperature year-round. Pete's going to try it tonight. You been there yet?"

"No, not this time."

"Oh, so you've been here before."

"Every spring for the past three years."

"You must really like it here. I could see why. How about you, Pete? Want to come back again next year on your spring break?"

The boy looked down at his camera. "If we can go back to the playa."

"How we going to do that, Pete? Remember, tour canceled? And forget taking one of those jeeps out." The woman stopped at the edge of the grass where the sidewalk began, at the 600 building. "Oh, this is us. Maybe we'll see you at the 49er or the general store. Pete and I, we go there after dinner to look at things, T-shirts and postcards, but don't buy the datenut bread—it's petrified. Practically had to chisel a piece off last night, didn't we, Pete? What else can you do here after dark? Anyway." She took Grace's hand and squeezed it. "When you visit you can pick out a cactus. Anything you want. Tall ones or short ones. Prickly. Not prickly. Well, I guess they're all prickly, except the succulents. Goodnight." She started climbing the steps up, the boy following.

Grace headed down the sidewalk, passing a family in their bathing suits and flip-flops, towels slung over their shoulders, and then looked over at the stables where the horses were gathered around troughs, in for the night. At her building she started up, but on the second step stopped short—the coyote was back, eating out of the garbage again. It got down, and to her astonishment, instead of running down the steps past her, escaping onto the golf course, it stepped through the open door, pausing to look back at her before disappearing into the hallway. She continued up the steps, pausing at the entry way, watching it trot past all the rooms down the long hallway to the other end where, stopping again, it craned its neck to look back at her before stepping through the open door, disappearing down the steps. At her room she slid the key in and opened it.

"That coyote just ran down the hallway." Grace looked at El-wood—he was sitting on the bed—and then back at the door.

Elwood shook his head. "That's why they should keep those doors shut. God knows what comes in here."

Grace took off her jacket and sat beside Elwood on the bed. "I'm sorry I'm late. We got a late start, and you were right—the weather was bad out there, but not as bad as you thought. The road was under construction too, so we got delayed. And our driver, well, he said they're canceling the tour." She kissed him on the cheek. "I met this nice woman and her son from Modesto. She lost her husband. But she still seemed happy."

"You left it open."

"What?"

"The door." Elwood got up and shut it. "What do you mean she was happy?"

"Not that her husband died of course. It was just that she didn't feel sorry for herself. That's all. But then again it's prob-ably easier to lose a spouse than a child. She invited us over to her place in Modesto."

"So you told her about Jared?"

Grace shook her head. "No, not exactly. There really wasn't any time."

"But you said she was happy."

Grace looked down at her feet, her sneakers still soggy from the Ubehebe. "We stopped at the crater. The wind was fero-cious there."

"I don't think we should keep coming back here anymore, not every year," Elwood said. "I don't see the point."

Grace took off her sneakers and looked at the dark gravel inside. "You should have come with me. The playa, the rocks, the mountains sloping up, all the Joshua trees. It was beautiful, even in the rain. Death Valley isn't the problem."

"Then what is?" Elwood said.

"Remember that couple from the grief therapy group, how they had to kick all those people out of their house? Complete strangers who'd crashed the funeral, even came back to the house and ate the food?"

"So what's your point?" Elwood said.

"You don't find that strange? Elwood, if you're angry because I went, just say so."

"Who said I'm angry? You're not making sense."

Grace put on a pair of sandals. "Look, I'm hungry. We had no lunch, only granola bars and water."

"You should have at least called to say you were going to be late."

"There was no way. The driver had a satellite phone, but it was only for emergencies. Let's skip the 49er and eat dinner at the Inn. Do something new."

"They won't let you eat in the dining room unless you're staying there. Maybe we can go tomorrow night and eat at the bar."

6

Stopped at another traffic light, Cody switched on his headlights. "Haven't made one yet. How's that possible?"

"Thanks for driving me," Stanley said.

"Well, you shouldn't be driving yourself, especially at night. Out of the hospital a day and already on the go. Why not wait awhile, at least till tomorrow? Hell, someone might shoot you for a prowler."

"'Coincidence is when God chooses to remain anonymous,'" Stanley said.

"Huh?" Cody started moving again.

"Over there on the church marquee all lit up." Stanley pointed out his window. "Bishop First Congregational. What do you suppose that means?"

"How would I know?"

"No, really."

Cody shook his head and sighed. "Okay. Give it to me again."

"'Coincidence is when God chooses to remain anonymous.'"

"Let's see. No accidents. Just sometimes the Big Man in the sky won't admit it. Pretty irresponsible in my book. Never been fond of religion."

"So you don't believe in anything?"

"Animals don't. Have you ever seen a giraffe pray? A cat go into church?"

Stanley chuckled. "If there's a mouse."

Cody started to slow down again, another red light ahead. "Now that's four. Maybe the Big Man's getting even with me." He pointed out the windshield. "See that all lit up? Now that's my kind of marquee. *Blade Runner*. Harrison Ford and the girl with the weird hairdo. What's her name?" The light turning, Cody started moving again. "Whatever happened to her?" He edged over to the right lane and then turned. "This it?" He switched on his brights and drove down a block. "Guess the city blew all its money on traffic lights."

"It's how people like it here. Dark. Like in Bridgeport. Less light, more stars. It's the one over there on the left. Just pull up."

Cody brought the car to a stop. "Is that how Bodie was—pitch dark?"

"Darker than dark."

"Sure you don't want help?"

Stanley took a twenty from his wallet. "Here. Grab a late dinner; then pick me up in an hour or so."

"That's a lot of burgers. Why don't we get dinner together and let this wait till next week? It's not easy, you know. Been through it myself."

"Yourself?"

"My wife."

"I didn't know you had one."

"Forty years ago in a canal in Davis where we used to live. That's where they found her car. Never found *her* though. A couple years later I finally cleaned out her stuff to give to Goodwill. But who wants to see your wife's clothes coming down the street on someone else? You know that's what the Mormons did after they settled in the west. They murdered the Fancher party. Killed the adults, adopted their children, and wore their parents' clothes. Of course the Mormons had it bad too. Persecuted as they were." Cody reached across to the glove compartment and popped it open. "Here." He handed Stanley a flashlight. "Electricity might be off. Don't forget your bags."

On the sidewalk, flashlight in hand, box of bags under his arm, Stanley watched Cody drive back up to Main Street. A dog started barking, the deep throaty bark of a large dog, but it seemed far off. Police cars, the Inyo County Coroner's van, yellow tape across the driveway, keeping back a small group of onlookers—that's how things had looked last time he'd been here nearly a year ago when they'd taken Lorna out. He walked up the driveway to the front porch and then reached into his pocket for the key, the piece of ribbon Lorna had looped through it, smooth and cool between his fingertips. He put the key in the lock and then hesitated, waiting for Lorna to flick the porch light on, for her to open the door, barefoot and laughing, and say, "Look at you picking my lock. Where's the black stocking?" She'd had the smallest teeth, baby teeth, little white squares. He remembered when she'd been just four years old falling off the backyard swing, breaking her arm, a little kid with a gigantic cast. He turned the key, and the lock turned over. He flipped the hallway switch, the light bright enough to see into Dell's room, the bed left as it was, blanket pushed down, pillow askew as if Dell had just gotten up and padded out to Lorna's room, on the wall the birthday present he'd given Dell last year, a train-shaped clock, its warning bars still crossing and uncrossing, the time—9:00 p.m.—still working. He went in, lifted the clock off the wall, and pulled out the battery. Then he continued down the hall, past the kitchen and dining room to Lorna's room, here most everything gone, likely taken as evidence, except for the bed frame and two pictures on the wall, pictures Lorna had taken from their father's house when he'd gone into *The Sonora*, charcoal portraits drawn when they were kids on a family vacation to San Francisco's Pier 39. Not those silly five-dollar street artist caricatures but serious portraits his parents had splurged on. Stepping up on the bed frame, he pulled those down too. Then he headed over to the closet and stopped short. **DO NOT ENTER!** A crude crayon drawing of a wolf atop a mountain was taped to it. Dell's, he assumed. He opened the door and pulled the cord. A bare bulb snapped on. Dresses on hangers, pants, sweaters—all her clothes were still here, tangled up in piles on the floor. He was amazed at it all, given that Lorna mostly wore the same thing—jeans and a sweater or sweats and a T-shirt. The last time he'd seen her in a dress was at their mother's funeral. Then his eye landed on a dark chest, partly buried under a pile of clothes. Kneeling down, he pulled the box toward him. It was heavy, a rusty key in its lock. His mother's good silver, he assumed, something else Lorna likely rescued from the house. He stood up and, scanning the upper shelves, spotted another box, this one of green cardboard. He pulled it down and inside found puffy white satin and lace, Lorna's old wedding dress. She'd worn it last Halloween and didn't look any different, a woman who never seemed to age. He put the lid back on and then started pulling clothes off hangers and off the floor and stuffing them in bags, filling half a dozen. Peering at them all lined up, he wondered why he'd bought black ones. That's what Lorna had been brought out in—a black body bag. Behind the police tape, he'd watched her rolled down the driveway, the gurney rattling like a broken shopping cart. Stanley pulled the cord and shut the closet door. **DO NOT ENTER!** He started pulling Dell's drawing off, but the edges started to tear, and so he began hauling the bags out instead and then the clock, the chest, the wedding gown, and finally the sketches. Waiting for Cody, he sat on the dark porch, listening to the distant sound of cars from Main Street. *Coincidence is when God chooses to remain anonymous.* There was something vaguely irritating about it, God letting Himself off the hook when it was convenient. Headlights coming down the street, Stanley stood up, grabbed two bags, and headed down the driveway.

Cody popped the trunk open. "All done?"

Stanley put the bags in. Then he headed up the driveway again, Cody following, both making a few trips.

"This the last of it, these paintings?" Cody asked, both of them on the porch again.

Stanley switched on the flashlight and shone it on the sketches. "Us as kids."

"Looks just like you before you messed up your face."

Stanley shifted the flashlight to Lorna's. "Lorna loved them, thought they were a perfect likeness, but the artist—he made us look too good, almost angelic."

"Well, he got her eyes all right," Cody said. "Who can say about the rest."

❧

On their way to dinner at the Inn, Elwood pulled his wallet off the nightstand and slid it in his back pocket. Grace put on a light sweater just in case it was chilly. After leaving the room, they walked down the hallway. At the steps, Grace paused, looking over at the garbage can. "Why don't they put a lid on it?"

Elwood shrugged and started down the steps. "Better garbage than campers' dogs, I guess."

"I'd think a coyote would find a fresh mouse tastier."

"But harder to get. Slim pickings out here." Elwood opened the car door.

"Good thing you weren't at the Ubehebe yesterday," Grace said, getting in. "You'd never get the door open."

"The driver let you get out there in a storm? No wonder they're canceling the tour." Elwood started the car and backed out.

Grace smiled. "We made him. It was on the itinerary. Not that anyone was dressed for it. But we got out anyway. Even the grandfather. A doctor. He took his grandsons. They'd never been to the crater before, and they wanted to see it. You know how people only go to a place once and never go back again."

As Elwood drove past the 49er Café, Grace looked at all the people milling on the veranda, if anyone from her group was there.

Elwood drove uphill toward the Inn, the white stucco, flagstone terraces, and forest of towering palms pitched up against the dusky sky. Elwood pulled into a gravel lot, into a spot facing a small succulent garden, a magenta bougainvillea climbing up a fan-shaped trellis. Out of the car, they entered at the very bottom of the Inn, walking single file through a long, pale-yellow tunnel, small bulbs hanging from the ceiling, lighting the way. At a set of wooden doors Grace turned to Elwood. "Is this the right way?"

Elwood pushed the doors open, on the other side a small gold-tarnished elevator.

"That was strange. You think that's an old mining tunnel?" She pressed the up arrow, and the elevator doors slowly parted.

"Hard to believe," Elwood said, following Grace in, "those tunnels so unstable and full of snakes."

"Or bears." The elevator jolted up.

"Bears?"

"Kamchatkan bears. A newspaper article I read while the car was being fixed," Grace said as the elevator came to a stop, and they stepped into the lobby and started walking down a hall, old black-and-white photographs of the inn and portraits of past park superintendents lining the walls and beneath them cases of turquoise Navajo jewelry for sale. As they passed the check-in counter, men in dark suits and women in long evening dresses strolled past or sat on rattan couches drinking wine, peering out the tall windows overlooking the darkening desert. Beyond the check-in counter, in a dark corner was the bar, and as they walked toward it a tall, gray-bearded man in a black turtleneck, a large silver crucifix hanging from his neck, walked by them, bowing slightly.

Elwood, pushing himself up on a stool, said, "Good. No one here. Thought it might be full."

Grace pulled out a stool and sank into the thick leather cushion. There were six of them running the length of the bar. She peered at the mirrored wall of colorful liquor bottles, thinking how only yesterday she'd been locked arm in arm with her fellow travelers at the crater's edge, soaked and shivering, in a tempest. The bartender, putting down two napkins, said, "Good evening, folks. What can I get you?" He spoke with a slight twang and was boyish-looking with bangs and a shock of straight dark hair, but the crosshatching at the corners of his eyes told Grace he was no kid. He wore a black vest over a white shirt but no name tag.

"You aren't from here, are you?" Grace said.

Smiling wryly, the man folded his hands in front of him and bowed slightly. "No, ma'am, I'm not. Most people aren't."

"We'd like to see the dinner menu," Elwood said.

The bartender reached under the counter and handed over two menus encased in burgundy leather, *The Inn at Death Valley* gold-etched into them.

"Any specials?" Elwood asked, opening his menu.

"They're tucked inside, sir."

"Where are you from?" Grace asked.

The bartender shrugged. "Nowhere really."

"So you don't actually have a home, a place you go back to?"

"Not anymore," the bartender smiled, "just move from park to park. Now what can I get you two to drink tonight?"

"Iced tea," Elwood said.

"A glass of wine, I think. Maybe a Zinfandel." Grace pushed the menu back to him. "So you like it that way, having no place to go back to?"

"Wouldn't have it any other way." Turning, he went to the register.

Grace, leaning toward Elwood, whispered, "Isn't that interesting? How old do you think he is?"

Elwood shrugged. "Too old to be drifting."

"But if you can make a living that way."

Elwood closed his menu. "I think I know what I want."

"Here we go." The bartender put their drinks down. "Take your time." He walked over to the register again, punched something in, and then walked out of the bar into the dining room.

Grace looked at her menu. "Are we expecting good weather for the trip back tomorrow?"

"Once we get over the pass and into the Central Valley it won't matter much," Elwood said.

"Well, what if we stayed longer," Grace said, recalling the flat, endless I-5 wasteland—the cow manure, the rest areas of vending machines and cinderblock bathrooms, and idling trucks. She hated that part of the trip.

"Here we go." The bartender put down a basket of bread swaddled in a white cloth and a small plate of butter, three perfect scoops. "Garlic parsley, maple nut, and chipotle chili. And of course our delicious datenut bread."

"So where do you go in the summer when the Inn closes?" Grace asked, spreading her napkin on her lap.

"Grand Canyon. My wife and I work the dining room at El Tovar and then come back in the fall when the Inn reopens. Fifteen years now. National Park nomads."

Elwood chuckled. "NPN. Is that a club?"

"No, sir. But there's lots of us. Now have you decided?"

"The salmon," Grace said.

"Short ribs," Elwood said.

"I'll put that right in."

"You see, he has a wife," Grace said.

"So?" Elwood said.

"Fifteen years and married. How can you call that drifting?"

Elwood pulled a piece of bread from the basket and, lifting the knife, he scanned the butter. "Where shall I start?"

Grace broke off a piece of datenut bread and couldn't help but think of the woman and her son chiseling away at the one they'd bought at the general store.

"How is it?" Elwood asked. He took a roll and started buttering it.

"Moist. Very fresh." Grace glanced to her left, over at the wall where a large, gold-framed painting hung, a horse-drawn wagon careening around a cliff's edge, the horses, recoiling, up on their hind legs, painted in dusty orange and brown hues. "I wonder why they hung it there in a corner? Dracula's castle. That's what it reminds me of. The trip there in the carriage careening around the cliff corner. You've seen it in the movies. At night, though."

"Where exactly is Dracula supposed to live? That looks like a frontier scene. The horses look terrified."

"The Carpathians. Hungary, I think."

"How do you know that?"

"It's in the book. Jared must have read it for school."

"How many of his books have you read?"

"I don't know. None really. Just a few here and there."

"How can you read a book here and there?"

A woman laughed. Grace turned back around and looked her way—a young blond woman in a white silk dress two stools over. Beside her, leaning into the bar, was an older white-haired man in a linen suit and bow tie. "She'll have a Blue Parrot," he told the bartender, "and I'll have an Addington." He spoke like an English actor from an old movie, Grace thought. "One ounce dry vermouth…"

"Sir, this is a full-service bar," the bartender said. "I know how to make everything."

"And one ounce sweet vermouth. Two ounces club soda with a twist of lime." He raised his finger and wagged it. "And this is important. Not in a highball class but a cocktail glass."

"A cocktail glass. Yes, very good, sir." The bartender turned to the register.

"It's Ashford, room 629," the man said, and then he turned to the woman, whispering something in her ear, and she laughed.

Grace had heard that sound before, the tinkering of glass, inviting and frightening, how the dark-haired woman from the enclave sounded, how Dracula's harem of female vampires laughed as they morphed from swirling dust to human figures, waiting to feed, and then back into dust.

"Oh, and excuse me." The man raised his finger again at the bartender. "And she'll have an appetizer too. The Little Gems with Devil's Gulch Rabbit."

The bartender, at the register, turned to face him.

"And," the man added, "give those people a drink. How sad they look."

"Oh, Lloyd," the woman said, "stop it." She looked over at Grace, dropped her chin, and smiled wanly, shaking her head. "He's so incorrigible. Completely hopeless. You must understand."

"Bartender, cancel the Addington," the man said. "Make them all Blue Parrots. Four all around."

"Very good, sir," the bartender said. "Four Blue Parrots it is." He started taking out glasses and turning them over.

"Oh no," Grace said. "We're not staying here. We have to drive, and, well, I already have this." She tapped her wine glass. "But thank you."

"Yes." Elwood raised his hand. "Thanks."

"Not in one of those ghastly trailer parks I hope," the man said.

"They're Winnebagos," the woman said, rolling her eyes, "some of them quite fancy. It's called camping."

"Very well." The man held up two fingers. "Bartender, make that two Blue Parrots. And have them delivered to room 629 along with the food." The man slipped his arm inside the woman's and started pulling her away.

"Are they drunk?" Grace said, watching them pass the check-in counter.

"Not yet," the bartender said, with a slight smile. Into a tall silver shaker he started pouring in various liquors and juices and then threw in a handful of sugar, finally adding crushed ice. After shaking it up, he poured the mixture into glasses.

"How pretty," Grace said. "What makes it so blue?"

"Curacao." The bartender carefully placed the glasses on a tray. "They used to crush beetles to get it that color, but now they just add food coloring."

After dinner, Grace and Elwood stepped out onto the flagstone terrace. Dark out now, the only light came from the Inn's windows, the flickering votives on the terrace tables, and in the distance red taillights winding down the road to the Ranch. The wind, having picked up, rattled the palms along the terrace.

"I could get used to that," Elwood said.

"It was good, but those people. That man. The way he spoke to the bartender."

"People here have money," Elwood said. "A lot of Hollywood types. I'm sure he's used to it."

"*She'll have a Blue Parrot.*" Grace imitated the man.

Elwood laughed. "He did offer us one."

"The way he dragged her across the lobby."

"Maybe she wanted to be dragged. Maybe they were practicing for a movie. Maybe he was a director."

"I doubt anyone wants to be dragged," Grace said.

"Well, the whole place is full of pretentious people. That's why you can't eat in the dining room if you're not staying here."

Walking down a series of dimly lit stone steps, they strolled around the grounds, weaving past various tiers of rooms and verandas to an observation deck, below it a long blue rectangular pool, a large black frond painted on its bottom—the Inn's motif, Grace assumed, having seen it on the menu cover and napkins.

"Such a lovely place. So peaceful. The fireplace too," she said. Made of stone, it burned orange, smoke swirling up into the sky, two men and a woman in white terry robes sitting around it.

"So whatever happened to Dracula?" Elwood said. "In the movies he always gets the stake through the heart, doesn't he? Or his coffin daylighted."

"In the book it's an act of mercy, not revenge. And despite all the horrible things he does—sucking people's blood, kidnapping babies to feed his harem—they feel sorry for him, the ones that hunt him down. When they stake his heart, he becomes human again. It's a very Christian book." A breeze came through. Sunken below the pool were more palms and a lush, steeply terraced garden. "Come on. Let's go down," Grace said, walking down a stone staircase to the very bottom where there were a series of ponds, lily pads floating on the surface.

"Wish I'd brought my camera," Elwood said.

Grace looked up at the rest of the tiered garden, another staircase cutting up the center, leading back up to the Inn. "Let's take that one," Grace said. As she started up, a ribbon of water, Furnace Creek she assumed, cascaded down alongside the staircase, while all around them a chorus of croaking began. Grace stopped and pointed. "Listen, Elwood, the children of the night. That's what Dracula called them. Of course he meant the wolves he let loose on those mothers pounding on the castle door."

"I don't remember any mothers in the movie," Elwood said, following Grace up.

"Wanting their babies back, the ones he snatched to feed his harem."

At the top now, they came to a large wooden door with wrought-iron handles.

"Now what?" Grace said.

"We could go back to the bar. Get dessert," Elwood said. "You can have a Blue Parrot."

"Or back to the room." Grace patted her purse. "Datenut bread—I took some with me. We have a long day tomorrow."

7

At 7:00 a.m. the next morning Stanley was already up, listening through his headset while readying the pool for the eventual Memorial Day onslaught.

Your faith was strong, but you needed proof
You saw her bathing on the roof.
Her beauty and the moonlight overthrew ya.
She tied you to her kitchen chair,
she broke your throne, and she cut your hair,
and from your lips she drew the Hallelujah.

"Leonard Cohen singing 'Hallelujah'," the DJ said. "Such a haunting song. Hundreds of remakes, maybe Jeff Buckley's best. A beautiful voice. Died in a freak accident, drowning." Last night, after Cody had dropped him off, helping him unload Lorna's stuff, Stanley had fallen asleep early for a change. If he'd dreamed about dragging Lorna through the woods, hauling her in and out, it had all evaporated come morning. Maybe there was something to that old wives' tale, the blow to the head, his concussion righting him. Or maybe cleaning out Lorna's closet had had some therapeutic value. Probably it was just a fluke. He peered into the empty pool. Crack patched, walls painted, it was ready to go. Now, slipping the hose in, he watched the water spread across the bottom. In a month or so when the season began, fishermen and families would arrive, the rivers running strong from the snowmelt. That's how he organized his life now—by seasons: spring brought the Fishers and their lost son; summer brought the fishermen and the families; fall brought the changing of the leaves; and winter, far quieter, marked Lorna's death. If it weren't for the pool and the motel backing the river, he probably would have gone bust, his motel being just another dumpy place without enough business. The kids loved the pool though, and their parents, those willing to spring for the larger rooms with decks off the river, loved the location. Water kept his business alive. Of course, it also killed, especially in spring. Three people had already died in Yosemite, he'd heard on the morning news, up at the top of Vernal Falls—one climbing over a guardrail for a picture and then slipping, another having gone over trying to save the first one, and then the third one trying to save the second one.

Letting the pool fill, Stanley walked back to the office, grabbing the newspaper—*The Mono News*. He scanned the headlines, "Mono Lake: A Lovely Place to Die," beside it a blurry picture of a young man riding a bicycle, his blond hair flying behind him.

> Wildlife biologists studying the reproductive cycles of seagulls found bones on a remote island in Mono Lake near Yosemite National Park. Testing of the remains revealed them to be that of Daniel Serrano, a twenty-one-year-old University of Wisconsin student who went missing over a decade ago. After failing to show up for his final exams, a friend went to his apartment and, finding the door ajar, called the police. After inspecting the apartment, authorities found no evidence of foul play. His car keys and wallet were on the kitchen counter along with a rent check and a stack of old, torn-up love notes. Only his bike was missing. Though Serrano's brother Glenn, an active member of NUM, the Network of the Unidentified & Missing, had always believed his brother to be a victim of foul play, Madison authorities considered Serrano a walkaway or a suicide, even though no suicide note was found at his apartment or on the island. How Serrano ended up on such a remote island is still a mystery.

Stanley went back in his unit and peered at the cinched garbage bags lined up against the wall. In the movies people always balled up their loved one's jacket or blouse, tearfully inhaling their scent, so he opened one up, but Lorna's clothes were all in a tangle—god knows how long she'd kept the stuff—so he cinched the bag back up and went back into the office, eyeing the newspaper again, the boy on his bike, blond hair flying behind him. Then into the computer he typed in NUM and up came the organization: *Giving the found their names and returning the missing to their families*, and below cases of the month and two small pictures, one a photograph of a little girl: Elly Goucher, eight years old, a chipped front tooth, last seen on May 10, 1978, in Whitefish, Montana, and the other, a sketch: Unidentified male, white, thirty to forty years old, found January 28, 1972, in Mayitville, Georgia. Stanley clicked on the sketch, and two larger versions of the man appeared, one with neck-length, curly dark hair tumbling across his forehead, the other with short, straight hair, both images containing the same wide-set eyes, long nose mushrooming at the bottom, and small-set mouth with thick lips:

> **Case File**: 5428MAL
> **Remains**: Skeletal
> **Height**: 5'8" to 5'9"
> **Eye Color**: Unknown
> **Clothing**: Blue jeans, a brown leather belt with a large brass belt buckle of a flaming bird, a T-shirt with the word *Phoenix* on it, blue socks, dark sneakers size 7-8, white paint splattered on them. Found sitting under a weeping willow tree on Highway 35 near Sebastian Road. No indication of foul play. Police believe he may have been waiting for someone and had a heart attack or been bitten by a snake.

The phone rang, but as he reached for it the ringing stopped, and then he noticed the light blinking—a message while he'd been out at the pool. Who would be calling so early? "Mr. Uribe, this is—" Recognizing the voice, he hit stop and then looked out his front window at a truck barreling by and then pressed play again. "Mr. Uribe, this is Dr. LeBeau, the Inyo County coroner. I don't know if you received my first message. I know you were hospitalized. But it's urgent that you contact me. I've talked to Sheriff Boyd. I understand you may be re-

luctant. I understand grief, Mr. Uribe. I've lost people too—"
Stanley pressed skip. "Hey, Stanley. It's me. I hope you're feeling
better—" He pressed stop. How many times had he played that
one, all of it less than a minute, all in Lorna's normal rhythms,
the message left three days before she'd died—he'd had a cold
then—the last syllable of each word rising as if she were perpetually asking a question. That's how she spoke. People who'd
never met her thought she was Chinese because of her rising
tone. That's why the end of the message, the single flat syllables
fading as if she were already pulling away, leaving, bothered him
the most. "Okay. Bye." Of course when he'd first gotten the
message he didn't think anything of it. She *was* leaving, that is,
probably pulling the phone away from her mouth as she spoke.
"Okay. Bye." But now those two small words haunted him,
despite what Sheriff Boyd had said at first, no doubt to com-
fort him, that she'd probably no idea what was coming. Poof!
Dead. But he knew that was only in the movies. He looked
at the two faces of the dead man. Heart attack or snake bite?
Neither made sense. Then he pondered what he'd told Lorna
all her life about her fears, every bump, every cancer. "Right
here. Can you feel it, Stanley? Please," she'd say when she was a
kid. "Is it cancer? Am I'm going to die? Feel it." And when he'd
said, no, she wasn't going to die, she'd keep asking that much
more urgently until she'd worn him down, and he'd lose his
patience, be mean, saying, "Yes, you're going to die," thinking
somehow just saying it might inoculate her against it or might
scare the fear out of her the way a sudden boo cured hiccups,
and his mother would scold him, saying, "Look what you've
done. Don't torment your sister. She'll grow out of it." But as
Lorna got older, the fear hadn't lessened, just evolved. Blood.
Contaminated blood. Hepatitis. AIDS. Malaria. She'd wrapped
Band-Aids around her fingertips just in case. After she had
Dell, though, she took medication to treat it, and, helping a
little, the medication lessened the endless questions, but still the
shadow followed her, the pointless doctor visits, all the medical
tests she'd persuaded them to do, and it eventually broke up her
marriage, he assumed.

Stanley went back into his unit, into the kitchen, over to the counter where he'd put the wooden chest he'd taken from her closet. He turned the key and lifted the lid, expecting to see sparkling forks and knives cradled in dark velvet—the good silver his mother brought out for the holidays—but rather it was a jewelry box. That no pink ballerina unfolded herself twirling slowly to Beethoven or Bach didn't surprise him. Lorna wasn't that type, nor did she wear much jewelry, just some small studs and a thin gold chain around her neck; still, the interior was more ornate, more feminine than he'd expected, the lid containing a large oval mirror in the center, two smaller oval glass picture slots framing it. Lorna hadn't slid any pictures in, though, so the original backing showed though, a delicate sketch of a wrought-iron chair, a teacup, and a fringed pillow, *Bombay Company* written in script above. Below, in the box itself, were four black velvet compartments of varying sizes, some containing a mishmash of discarded jewelry—earrings, necklaces, bracelets, and other things. He picked up a small silver barrette that looked like a child's, a fine silver mesh woven into an intricate leafy pattern, a tiny diamond in the center. It could have been an antique, Victorian maybe. Lorna had been a beautiful baby, very small with delicate features, porcelain skin, a fine web of veins, and large, bright eyes, a dusting of hair. He'd been twelve at the time, and he'd gotten the impression that Lorna had come as a surprise to his parents, the result of something gone wrong. He remembered seeing her in the hospital nursery, sometimes serene, eyes staring up dreamily at the ceiling as if doves were fluttering, a pink bow on her head, other times, her face contorted, tear-stained, tiny pink fists beating air. He looked back down into the jewelry box. Another compartment held a menagerie of glass figurines: an owl, a mantel clock with silver feet, a branch with two orange-beaked parrots, a seal, a sitting dog, a seashell, and a starfish. These, too, he'd never seen before, though the seashell and the starfish reminded him of the printouts Sheriff Boyd had brought him, the strange coral-like configurations. He started organizing jewelry, separating the earrings, matching up the mates. The few pairs he could match he put back in the compartment. The orphaned earrings, stuff Lorna hadn't bothered to throw away, he scooped up and slid in a plastic bag. Those he'd throw away later. He shut the lid and then went back into the office, where Cody was behind the counter now looking at the computer. "What's this? These pictures. This wooden man."

Stanley reached over and closed the site. "What are you doing here so early?"

"Well, at least your face looks better than his."

Stanley rubbed his cheek.

"Those stitches still holding you together, like Frankenstein, huh?"

"Like the creature. Frankenstein was the doctor that put him together."

Staring absentmindedly, Cody said, "Young, not half bad looking, smart, and no wife."

"Actually he was pretty hideous looking. That's what caused all the trouble. The creature wanted a wife, one that looked like him."

"I was talking about you."

"I still have a wife. Hasn't divorced me yet. But the creature never got that far. Ran off to the far reaches of the earth. Anyway, you don't need to worry about me."

"Who said I was? It's Miguel. He took down his sign. He's changing the name of his restaurant."

"Is he? The old woman won't like that. Didn't she start the business?"

"Yeah, but his mother hasn't left the house for years. Plus the world has changed—you know, more international, especially in August when all the foreigners flood in, the nutty ones heading for the desert."

"Don't knock the foreigners. We need them."

"Says he wants to make it sound less Mexican, thinks he'll attract more tourists that way. But he'll still serve Mexican."

"Very clever. So what's he going to call it—the Jones Restaurant?"

Cody chuckled. "Doesn't sound very appetizing, does it?"

"I'm going to check the pool." Stanley stepped outside, but the pool was only halfway there. He'd forgotten how long it took. He should have started earlier. He went back to the office.

"Done?"

Stanley shook his head. "Can't rush water."

"No doubt about that. You decide what you're going to do with Lorna's stuff?"

"Was that really true what you told me about your wife?"

"Why wouldn't it be? You think I'd make something like that up? Well," Cody said, "maybe I'll stop over at Miguel's after I close up tonight before he goes all fancy. Say, are refried beans really Mexican?"

"What makes you think they aren't? Remember I'm Basque. My family's from northern Spain, not Mexico."

"They're both Spanish speaking though, right?"

"Say, if Miguel really does change the name, get some new menus for the front desk. He's the only one that stays open late." He was thinking of the Fishers arriving late, the only guests he really cared about. It'd be another year before he'd see them again, assuming they kept coming up. They might just move on. But move on where? He knew it wasn't that simple, that even Frankenstein's creature, despite its fury at its creator for refusing to create a wife, wept over Frankenstein's dead body.

Stanley went back in his unit, into the kitchen, and opened the jewelry box again. As he started to pull out the plastic bag of orphaned earrings, the ones he'd planned on tossing, he noticed two looped ribbons on either side of the velvet shelf. Inserting his fingers in the loops, he gently lifted the shelf, discovering another compartment; in it, he found various objects, a fragment of mirror, a thick silver wire bent into a circle, a choker of some sort, he assumed, and another glass figurine, this one larger, a carousel, damaged, the horses and poles chipped. And then he pulled out a large oval brush, the back of it silver, tarnished and chipped too, the sort you might find in a lady's old-fashioned toilet or a Jamestown antique store. Turning it over, he saw spooled up in the pale bristles, hair, lots of it, reddish, fine and straight, hair he'd seen so many times in his dreams as he slid Lorna in and out, moving her from one place to another in the dark woods. He felt the back of his neck go cold. He looked around the room, at what was up against the wall—the black garbage bags, the sketches, their childhood faces looking back at him, and then over at the angels gliding back and forth across the tank, pursing and unpursing their lips. He lifted the brush to his nose; it smelled slightly sour, like milk, and then he pulled out a strand and held it to the light. He'd read about some finds in the southwest, cliff dwellings, pottery, bones found in slot canyons, wedged between narrow crevices, how Indians believed disturbing the dead or dreaming about them meant their ghosts were rising up from the underworld.

Stanley put the brush back and gently closed the lid and then grabbed his sunglasses and car keys. He stepped into the office. "Going to see my father, Cody. Keep an eye on the pool, will you?" In his truck, Stanley turned onto 395. It was nice being alone, behind the wheel again, moving through space, out of town into ranchland, but he knew it wouldn't last, the pleasant post-recovery euphoria, the night of solid sleep he'd just had, and that dopamine boost Caitlin once talked about in patients who'd cheated death or gotten transplants, claiming they'd been reborn, could feel the donor's spirit beating in them. But now turning onto Highway 108 and starting to climb into dense forest, he thought again about the man he'd left behind, the man from the hospital, in the bed beside his. The hospital wouldn't keep him forever; eventually he'd end up in a nursing home. Or maybe not. Maybe the next time his phone rang or the message light was blinking it would be that man, taking him up on his invite: a river view room and fishing, even though Stanley himself didn't fish, and then to Miguel's for a beer and Mexican food. Of course, for all he knew the man might be a drunk, like Rusty, the guy he'd bought the motel from, or a rich guy never staying in a dump like his. But that didn't seem likely since rich guys probably got visitors, lots of them, and didn't end up in a small foothill hospital in a double room.

An hour later, Stanley approached the pass; the lot empty, he headed down to Strawberry, passing the inn where he and

Caitlin had stopped for a drink, his whole life one small circle. But it was a beautiful one, he thought, surrounded by forest, the road to himself for the moment. He didn't mind all the driving, the only sound the rumble of his engine as he came down through Long Barn and Mi-Wuk, the road widening in Twain Harte where there was traffic. Soon he was at Sonora, pulling into the nursing home lot. Peering in the rearview mirror, he wondered if his father would recognize him, his face still tight, stiff, and sutured. In the rearview mirror he smiled at himself, trying to make himself feel human. *I understand grief, Mr. Uribe. I've lost people too,* Dr. LeBeau, the coroner, had said, trying to sound human.

Out of the truck now, he walked down the steps beneath the canopy and into the lobby, and signed in. He took off his sunglasses, trying to adjust to the shifting of the light, from sunlight to dim purple florescence. He peered at the pale walls and the faded floral wallpaper runner around the room's perimeter. But something was different about the runner this time, the leaves on the flowers greener as if someone had colored them in, leaving the petals for another day. Or maybe his eyes were playing tricks on him. A concussion could distort his sense of smell, his ability to organize his thoughts, Dr. Katz had said. There might be headaches, anxiety. Residual damage to the brain was little understood and often didn't show on scans and so on. He might not be the same person. But then again maybe the concussion could have the opposite effect, sharpening his senses, his sense of smell, which unfortunately, hadn't left him. Food, disinfectant, shit—no one odor distinct—the smell wasn't pungent enough to be putrid but merely unpleasant and elusive, a mealy perfume you could never get rid of.

Off to the right was a couch, a few chairs, and a brick fireplace, two faux tree-like plants framing it, and some *AARP, Sports Illustrated,* and *Good Housekeeping* magazines fanned out across a coffee table, and to the left, the reception desk, an old woman behind it talking on the phone. As he signed in, she didn't even look up. Passing the dining room, which was empty—the down time between lunch and dinner—he saw the large TV inside it, elephants lumbering across the screen. He headed toward the elevator, a large double, which could easily accommodate two gurneys, and rode up. After exiting, he approached the locked doors. Same mural, same caged bird, same words *This Way* greeted him as he waited to be buzzed in. "Glad to see you back, Mr. Uribe," the nurse said. "We lost two souls while you were away. Nathan was one, so your father has a new roommate. Frank Holiday. A young man. Brain damaged. Sometimes he screams, and it upsets your father. We didn't tell him about your accident. Between everything else and his hallucinations. The little men waking him up, turning off his TV, hanging up the phone on him. I assume your wife told you. But the good news is they seem to have disappeared. At least for today. Your father will be glad to see you."

Stanley headed down the hallway, passing food carts stacked with lunch trays and on the other side wheelchairs, some empty, some with bodies flopped over or upright. He kept his gaze down on the footrests, some feet bare, some socked, until he reached the Frozen Man's room—he'd almost forgotten about him—and to his surprise saw only a bare mattress, sun streaming in from the lifted shade. In his father's room now, he walked around Nathan's bed, empty too but, blanket rumpled, pillow creased, clearly slept in. Walking around it, Stanley pulled back the curtain. *Quite agile, elephants can cover up to 120 miles a day in search of water.* Stanley picked up the remote and turned the sound down.

"Hey." His father frowned. "What are you doing? I was watching that. I told you not to come back, stupid little man."

"Dad, it's me. Your son, Stanley."

His father pointed toward the curtain. "Shh. He's a screamer."

"Your new roommate? Looks like he's out for the day." Stanley pulled the curtain closed.

"Nathan died. When the dog came by, he fed it biscuits." He pointed to the curtain. "But he's a screamer. It's true." His father glared at him. "Say, are you really my son? The nurse said my son was coming."

"I am. Promise."

"Well, something bad happened to him," his father said. He folded his hands on his stomach. "A spy, a Nazi. That's what he said I was."

"Nathan? Wasn't he a fighter pilot in WWII?"

"He threw all his food in the garbage."

Stanley heard someone come into the room, feet shuffling, and then a familiar voice, the Jamaican accent, his father's main aide, Patrice. "Okay, Mr. Holiday, back you go." He heard the grind of the Hoya lift, a swing-like contraption to hoist bed-ridden people. "A quick change now and time for your nap." Stanley heard the bed rails fold down and felt the curtain flutter behind him. Then came a series of shrieks, high-pitched like a girl's, and then an elongated "Oooww." And then, "You're hurting me, bitch," in a deeper, slower, angrier voice and the terrible smell. Stanley tried to hold his breath while his father, squeezing his eyes shut, covered his nose with his hand.

"Shame on you, Mr. Holiday. Now say you're sorry," Patrice said.

"Sorry. Bitch."

"Be nice now," Patrice said, "so I can get you all neat and clean."

Stanley picked up the remote and turned the sound back up. *Rarely ever seen, the elusive snow leopard makes its home in the remote Himalayas,* a man in a parka and thick gloves crouched in a lookout in a snowy mountain landscape on the screen now.

His father opened his eyes again.

"You're a nice girl," the man's voice said, now calm and slurry, almost childlike, as if he were silly drunk.

"Well, you're nice too, Mr. Holiday," Patrice said. "See? It's not that hard. You don't want to be all messy, do you?"

"My name's not messy. It's Howie."

Patrice laughed. "That's not your name, silly."

"Silly's my name." He snickered.

"Time for your nap now, Mr. Holiday. Nighty night."

Behind him Stanley felt the curtain shift, and as Patrice pulled it back and stepped through, he got a quick look at the man, his puffy face, dark scallops of hair around his ears a man-size baby in a junior bed, before Patrice pulled the curtain closed again.

"Well, well, look who's here. Your son, Mr. Uribe."

His father shook his head. "Don't blame me. I'm no Nazi."

"Of course you're not, Mr. Uribe." Patrice pulled off her gloves and threw them in the garbage.

"Nathan died," his father said.

"That's right," Patrice said, "and we're all very sad."

"He didn't like the food."

"Well, we don't have to worry about that since you're such a good eater. And your son's here to visit."

"Well, it stinks," his father said.

"I know," Stanley said, glancing back at the curtain.

"The food. Haven't you been listening?"

Patrice put on a new pair of gloves. "Time for your bath now, Mr. Uribe. Your son can wait outside. It won't take long."

"Dad, I'm going to take off now, but I'll be back for another visit soon." Stanley stepped around the curtain.

Tucked in and quiet now, the man lifted his hand, saying meekly, "Bye," as Stanley walked around the foot of his bed.

Back in his truck now, pulling out of the lot, Stanley headed back to 108, though he was thinking of detouring over to his father's old house first—sold to pay for his father's care at the nursing home—something he sometimes did, especially after Lorna had died. But today he got directly onto 108, heading up into the forest, conjuring the house up in his mind instead, the brown-shingled, yellow-shuttered raised ranch, the driveway where his parents parked the station wagon, the Ford Squire, the very car that he drove in his nightmares through the dark woods, Lorna on the deck. Upstairs were all the bedrooms—Lorna's with green shag carpet, hot pink walls; then downstairs was a small, windowless, wood-paneled den, a little cave off the playroom he'd eventually moved into so he and his teenage friends, door closed, could sip beer and flip through *Playboy*. But Lorna, who'd always hung out with them in his upstairs bedroom, had punished him for it; *Lost in Space* was on the play-

room TV that day, a show they used to watch together about
a family trapped on a desolate planet with a talking robot that
waved its arms frantically, shouting, "Danger! Danger!" Then
from inside his room, he and his friends had heard her suddenly start screaming, "Stop. Stop it! You're hurting me, Stanley!"
loud enough that his father, upstairs, had come halfway down,
yelling at him to knock it off or get a beating.

Approaching Mi-Wuk now, Stanley heard the grind of an
engine close behind. In his rearview mirror he saw a deer in
the truck's bed, and he sped up, but the truck, still on his tail,
was honking now. He hated these kinds of people: somewhere
to get, no time to get there; or nowhere to get, no time to get
there. And he thought of making him wait until Twain Harte
where the road briefly widened to two lanes, but then the last
thing he needed was another accident or a run-in, so he—a man
going nowhere, plenty of time to get there—moved off to the
side. But then again if Dr. LeBeau and Sheriff Boyd were to be
believed that wasn't exactly true. But for now, the hunter having
passed, he, alone in the forest again, took his time, and some
two hours later he was back at the motel well before he needed
to be on duty.

"How'd the truck do?" Cody asked.

"Fine," Stanley said, walking around the counter and opening the door to his unit. "I'm going to lie down for a while." On
his bed Stanley stared up at the ceiling, a spider crawling across
it, starting and stopping, eventually lodging itself in a corner.
In early fall, before the cold came, they spun crazy webs down
by the river, some webs concentric circles, others haphazard,
a mishmash. He'd seen a documentary on the brown recluse,
its flesh-eating venom. But you had to search the dark hidden spaces to find it, attics or long-forgotten sheds. Get your
flashlight on it, and still the spider, wanting no trouble, would
scramble off. As Stanley's eyes closed, a voice started calling
out to him: *Hey, Stanley. What are you doing here?* Crouched down
at his high school locker, shuffling though papers, he suddenly
realized it was Lorna annoying him, crowding him, and somehow she *was* alive! But how could that be? Then, bell ringing,

she suddenly vanished in a crowd of kids moving through the hallway, and, trying to keep sight of her, he ran frantically after her, weaving in and out of the crowd, the back of her head disappearing while he shouted, "Wait! Wait!" Then, suddenly, he was alone at the bottom of a dank lightwell, on the ground a tiny white figure, a miniature doll, which he picked up and to his astonishment felt move. Elated, he ran up the stairs to a landing where two girls, books pressed to their chests, stood beside a sunny window. But when he opened his hand to show them, the girls just giggled, and he saw what it really was, just a plastic figurine, discolored, forgotten, a piece of junk that somebody had thrown away.

Their last day, Grace woke at sunrise and packed while Elwood slept. Then she slipped out of the room. At the top of the steps, beside the garbage can, she surveyed the half-full parking lot. It was pleasantly cool and quiet, the only thing quieter than the early morning desert was the quiet of a dead child's bedroom. She'd been in enough of them, the few invitations she'd accepted from the grief therapy mothers, always starting with coffee, ending with a neatly made twin bed, stacked schoolbooks on a desk, postered walls, maybe a music stand, a score on it, in the corner, a dark violin or flute case, dust motes floating in the sun rays that managed to squeeze through the shut blinds. Grace turned a little, looking back through the open door down the dim hallway of closed doors to her own, 842, Elwood behind it, and then went down the steps.

As she got in the car, a bird started squawking loudly, one of those long-tailed black birds, a grackle, glaring down at her from a tamarisk. They were all over the park, those birds, and could make a terrible racket. Grace shut the door, hoping it would stop. *Be back soon.* She'd left a note on the nightstand. It wasn't like she was leaving for good though—leaving doesn't suddenly happen in one big step like in the movies.

Driving through the lot now, she passed the 600 building where the woman and her son were staying, the grassy area and pool, and then the 49er Café, a few people on its veranda, waiting for the doors to open. Then she turned onto the road, passing the gas station, then the ranger station, traveling the same route the van had yesterday, though today she'd be heading toward Stovepipe Wells, the way she and Elwood had come in. She knew she could have waited for Elwood, that if she asked he would stop on their way out as he had last year, but anxious about the long haul home today—they always drove back without overnighting—he would have rushed her. And she didn't blame him. Once out of Death Valley and into the valley, it was endless hours on I-5 eventually in the dark with few exit spots.

Passing the turnoff to Mustard Canyon, Grace now saw the valley open up before her. Next came the Beatty Cutoff, and after passing it she slowed down, turning left onto a washboard road—a far cry from Racetrack Road—pot-hole free and wide enough to pass an oncoming car. But still the car rattled, and in her rearview mirror she could see sand whirling up, the rock, mostly pebbles, crunching beneath her tires. Only two other cars in the lot, she pulled into a spot near a gray picnic table. A crow, perched on it, took flight, cawing. Despite the narrow stream here, Salt Creek was one of the hottest parts of the park, sweltering in the full sun of day, a blinding bright light. But now the sun was still dull, gently warming the land, lighting the rocks up in various hues. She stepped up onto the boardwalk that wove through the marsh, the shallow stream running alongside it. Beneath her feet the blond planks creaked slightly as she walked along, gazing down at the pup fish, sand-colored, guppy-sized, blending in with the sandy bottom, with a good bit of scalloped fin. Crouching down, she watched them shoot up tributaries, invading each other's dens, each guarding its small pool, vigilantly chasing off intruders, tails swishing frantically. A solitary, exhausting life as far as she could tell, they were tough fish, the only ones that could survive such a salty brine. In fact, she could smell the salt. Mildly acrid, it wasn't unpleasant.

She kept walking, passing a few people, who greeted her with a pleasant hello. Halfway in now, she paused at a lookout, where the stream widened into a pool and ran deeper, its sandy banks full of pickleweed; then she continued out to the farthermost point, where the boardwalk started to circle back. There the rest of the valley wandered off, continuing between two banks of rock, one grayish green, the other rust, in between a sandy, moist mix of grass and reedy marsh. This is where Jared must have wandered off, what he might have been describing in his postcard, the only one that had arrived. *Great place. Hot though. Lots of pup fish. Went off trail. More water, reeds. A lone duck. Horse flies. Ouch! Ran back.* She and Elwood hadn't ever gone off the boardwalk—it was a big step down—but clearly others had. She could see their footprints now in the moist sand making their own trails.

The step down was steeper than she'd expected, or maybe it was because the sand was damper than she'd expected, her feet sinking deeper. After steadying herself, she took a few steps and then looked behind her, back at the boardwalk, but no one was there, just the planked walkway, the sunlit valley, the muted brown, green, burgundy rock beneath a pale blue sky. This was the way leaving began. All the footprints, some small enough to be children's, told her this. But it was a well-traveled trail. Nothing to be afraid of. She thought of the painting at the Inn's bar, the terrified faces of the passengers as the carriage careened around the cliff as the sun set, and she thought of the way the book ended, a sentence Jared had scribbled down on a scrap of paper: *The Castle of Dracula now stood out against the red sky, and every stone of its broken battlements was articulated against the light of the setting sun.* And she knew that no matter how far out she wandered, the prints would lead her back.

She walked out a ways amidst the pickleweed and salt grass, the brine stronger here, the sand wetter, and then came upon a thick patch of reeds and tall grasses, as Jared had described, and then she heard something in the distance, the preoccupied chatter. Surely it couldn't be the very same duck Jared had described, could it? But still she marveled at the idea, at the sound of it, so different from the irritating screech of the grackle. Trying to pinpoint its whereabouts, she peered into the reeds,

turning every once in a while to look back at where she thought
the boardwalk might be, her point of reference. She knew
distance and sound could be deceptive, the desert drawing
you out, and her feet were sinking deeper with each step, the
moisture creeping into her sneakers. If she went any farther,
she'd be ankle deep in sandy muck. Quicksand in the desert?
She'd never heard of such a thing. Something pinched the back
of her leg, right through her pants, and she let out a cry. Then
came another, and she whipped around. Horse flies? She was in
the right place but dared not take another step! She heard the
chattering again, close by, but no matter which way she moved,
she knew she'd be bitten again. Retreating would be better; it
was probably all the moisture that attracted the flies, yet the
duck was close by. She could still hear it. She took two steps
forward and felt another sharp pinch on her other calf, and she
swung around, looking for the culprit, rubbing the back of her
leg. Standing still again, she continued scanning the reeds, the
pain from the bite starting to subside, and she suddenly saw
it, just for a second, swim by, its emerald throat between the
burgundy reeds. She took a step back and waited. This was how
she'd have to move, one slow step at a time, in slow motion,
tricking the flies. Finally, when the ground became firmer, the
reeds receding, she turned and picked up her pace. Ahead was
the boardwalk, an old couple on it. The man in a straw hat, a
pair of binoculars around his neck, leaned over and offered her
a hand up.

"You lost?" the woman asked.

"More pup fish?" the man asked, looking down the path.
"Sign says they fight so much they're nearly extinct."

"And the eggs have to hatch all by themselves," the woman
said.

"More water and a duck. Horseflies too," Grace said.

The man raised his binoculars.

"You have to get in close and wait," Grace said. "He's all by
himself."

The man lowered his binoculars and chuckled. "A recluse."

His wife laughed. "What about those ducks on the golf

course, in the water holes. He need not be a lonely duck unless he wants to."

"You want to go out there?" The man gestured to the trail and then looked at his wife.

"And get bit?" She turned to Grace. "And your feet all wet."

Grace peered down at her sneakers. They were coated with sand.

"And plenty to see right here," the woman said and then turned to Grace. "Well, you have a nice day."

The man lifted his hat. "Yes, it was nice meeting you." Then they turned and started back down the boardwalk. When they were halfway back, Grace followed, and then some thirty minutes later she was back in the room, Elwood packing his suitcase.

"Where were you?" he asked.

"On a walk. I woke up early."

Elwood shut his suitcase.

"Don't worry. I'm already packed. We can just leave the keys in the room this time. Get out early." Grace laid her key on the dresser.

"You don't want to stop at the check-in counter, see the Indian woman?"

Grace picked up her suitcase and headed to the door. "There might be a line, and who knows if she's working. I'll see her next time."

Elwood followed her out and closed the door. At the car he loaded the luggage and then got in. After passing through the lot, they were on the road heading back out of the park, and before too long they were passing Salt Creek, then Devil's Cornfield, the Mesquite Sand Dunes, and then Stovepipe Wells. Climbing up into the Panamints, they'd eventually head down to Trona and Ridgecrest and then up through the Tehachapis and finally down to Bakersfield to pick up I-5, the quicker route home.

"Here we go," Elwood said.

INDIAN FLAVORS. Grace peered up at the towering sign near the highway on-ramp, on it, a caricature of a grinning

man in a red turban holding a giant ladle. Then, out of Bakersfield, orchards, cornfields, feedlots, and the smell of dung and
chemicals hung in the air beneath a brownish-blue haze. Two
hours later, Elwood pulled into a rest stop, one of only a few,
California making its weary drivers suffer long stretches before
letting them off. The lot full, Elwood drove slowly through
while Grace looked over at the people milling near the vending
machines and filing in and out of the restrooms.

"Here we go." Elwood pulled into a spot, and Grace opened
her door, careful not to hit the car beside her where two men,
slouched down, baseball caps over their faces, were dozing.
Grace stepped up on the curb and wandered over to a glass
case, inside a large glossy I-5 map, where people were tracing
their routes.

"I know where we're going," Elwood said, coming up behind her.

"I know. You go ahead." She nodded toward the restrooms.
"Let's meet over at the dog park." Grace moved away from the
people over to another smaller case, this one with black and
white flyers, these with the California State Attorney's Office
seal stamped on them, children's faces. One, a curly-haired girl
with tiny teeth and a quizzical smile, caught her attention.

Katie Castle, Age 10
4'8" 85 Pounds
Blue Eyes, Brown Hair
Last Seen April 10, 1997 in Lone Pine, CA

Grace scanned all of the faces. Each year she'd always made
a point to. No one else seemed to. Then she spotted another
flyer with a list of last year's statistics for all the state's missing.

Lost	350
Catastrophe	41
Stranger Abduction	15
Suspicious Circumstances	513
Unknown Circumstances	3,073
Voluntary Missing	35,722
Dependent Adult	2,003

Lost, a person who strayed away, was how the authorities wanted to tag Jared, but she and Elwood had argued for *Suspicious Circumstances*, likely abduction with no witnesses, thinking it would be given higher priority, and back then Grace truly believed Jared had been kidnapped, despite what the rangers had told her that first trip out about young men, thinking themselves invincible, being the most likely to get in trouble, take chances. *Lost*. But what intelligent, healthy young man couldn't find his way *back*? Plenty, she knew the rangers would say, the desert outsmarting the smartest, the healthiest. And now that she better understood the desert's pull, how Bram had to drag the boy off the playa as the storm grew worse, how foolish even she'd been agreeing to climb the Ubehebe's wind-torn edge, she thought the rangers might have been right. Or maybe not. Maybe Jared had staged it all, V*oluntary Missing*, an adult runaway, one of Castaneda's women picking him up, driving him to Castaneda's LA home, the whole gang hiding in plain sight. But that was the stuff of movies or one of Castaneda's books, wasn't it? And now Castaneda was dead.

Grace stepped away from the case, walking past the vending machines over to the restrooms. A series of endless silver stalls, toilets flushing, doors swinging open and closed, women two at a time washing their hands at the metal sinks, the constant whirring of hand dryers, it felt like a prison. She stepped inside a stall, shut the door, and to her surprise saw a face looking back at her, a boy, maybe fourteen or fifteen, Asian, with a stern expression, thick lips. A mesh vest covered his torso, on his head, a pointed cap. His face—stiff, wooden, fierce—didn't look particularly human but like a rendering, a mask, yet at the same time his eyes seemed human enough, looking right at her, imploring her.

MISSING

2,312-year-old-male. Speaks no English. Was last spotted boarding an airplane with a small army departing from China to San Francisco. Complexion: Muddy and chipped. Please help us find him. Reward.

Was this some sort of hoax? She peered at the phone number at the bottom and then pulled the flyer off the stall door and put it in her bag and walked out. Heading toward the grassy area, she saw Elwood near a chain-link fence, on the other side a cornfield, not Devil's Cornfield, but a field of real corn in real sheaves growing from real stalks.

"There you are," Elwood said.

Grace looked at the sign hanging on the fence: *Watch Your Step. Rattlesnakes.* "You'd think they'd be more concerned about dog poop. We've never seen a snake here, have we?"

"Well, maybe they've seen you."

Grace peered over the fence, the stalks far taller than her, packed in tightly, going back as far as she could see. "Out there I don't see how you *couldn't* run into one."

"All done by machine now, the picking, I bet," Elwood said. "Speaking of which do you want something from the vending machines before we leave?"

"How far to Santa Nella?"

"Not too," Elwood said.

"Then I guess we should wait."

"Eat at Janssen Pea? Unless you want to stop at the Smith Ranch, pick out your own cow." Elwood chuckled.

She remembered last year, passing the place, the foul smell, how one lone cow, having escaped the masses, stood atop a dung heap. "What a dreadful place."

"It's the economic powerhouse of California. Puts food on the plate."

Grace looked up at the brown haze; she found it hard to believe only hours ago she'd been beneath the blue sky of Death Valley. But it was all the same sky, wasn't it? "It smells bad."

"You say that every year. You can't live your life in a national park."

"People do."

"And live where?"

"They give you housing."

"You, in a trailer in the enclave? The woman who never stepped foot in the desert, probably never would have, and now you want to live in a rusted-out trailer behind the motel? That's a fantasy. And what about Duke—you going to let a cat run around the desert?"

"He'll eat lizards."

"Or get eaten by coyotes. Come on, let's go," Elwood said, turning away from the fence.

Stanley got off the bed, the bittersweet dream—the white, gauzy doll, those girls laughing at him—still hanging over him, and Lorna's voice: *Hey, Stanley. What are you doing here?* Why ask him that? Why *wouldn't* he be in school at his locker shuffling papers? What was *she* doing there? The dream didn't make sense, Lorna not even old enough to be in high school at the same time he was. He looked at the clock: 1:00 p.m. He'd only slept for half an hour. He went out to the counter. "You can close up early. I have to go out again."

"Again?" Cody shook his head. "Didn't you just come back from seeing your father?"

"I'm fine. Go ahead. We have no check-ins. We'll be busy enough come Memorial Day."

"How you ever going to recover running around so much?"

"I just had a nap. Never felt better."

"Well, you look like hell." Cody came out from behind the counter and slipped on his jacket. "You sure?"

"I'm fine. Really." Stanley went behind the counter and turned on the No Vacancy sign.

"Remember I'm off tomorrow," Cody said, walking out the door.

Stanley pulled out the autopsy report, jotting down the coroner's address on a scrap of paper, and then went out to his truck. Radio on, he got back on 395. "Jim Morrison up next in our countdown of huge talents dying before their time. 'Riders on the Storm.' Morrison's last song supposedly based on serial killer Billy Cook, a bad dude who posed as a hitch hiker, making his victims drive him around for days before doing them in. So if you're on the road today, especially if it's dark and stormy, be

careful." The song started, and when Morrison finally began
singing Stanley sang softly along with him, the only Doors song
he knew the lyrics to, though he could never make full sense
of them, except they seemed gloomy, Morrison's deep, distant
voice whispering the lyrics, the backdrop, the sound of tires
swishing through rain, the rumbling of thunder. He'd always
thought the song might be about a killer, a driver prowling the
side of the road for victims, but now he realized to his horror it
was really about a family on a road trip picking up a hitch hiker,
the killer himself. As Morrison's voice trailed off and only the
eerie sound of rain remained, the DJ came back on. "Okay,
well, just fooling. Didn't mean to scare all you folks out there
on the road today. No worries, Cook long gone, executed at San
Quentin." Stanley turned off the radio.

Coming down Conway Summit, Stanley could see all of
Mono Lake, such a lovely blue-green today that he thought of
turning onto Cemetery Road, having a brief visit with Lorna.
But instead he kept driving, determined to get it over with, go
see Dr. LeBeau, as the turnoff to the cemetery slipped behind
him in his rearview mirror. Up ahead was Lee Vining, then the
Pantum Crater, a rocky, barren place most tourists skipped,
then June Lake and Mammoth Lakes, but he kept the wheel
straight for miles until the road finally started dropping into
Owen's Valley, and he was back in downtown Bishop, on Main
Street again stopped at a light, McDonald's to his left, church
to his right where the message had changed: *We are drawn to a
thing because it's good; it enslaves us when it becomes necessary.* Looking
in his rearview mirror, he wondered if anything was necessary.
He'd never even called Dr. LeBeau back; no appointment, he
might as well turn around, but then the light changed and he
was moving again, up ahead a sign catching his eye: *Better Homes
& Gardens.* He hung a right only to find the same sign in front
of Lorna's house with a *Please Don't Disturb the Residents* added
to it, and a high-heeled woman in a polka-dotted dress coming
briskly down the driveway as he got out.

"Arlene Vega," she said slightly out of breath, reaching for his hand, "the realtor here, but I'm afraid you're just a tad early. Open House not for an hour. But isn't she sweet? Owner's anxious to sell. If you could come back—"

"I heard someone died here" slipped out of his mouth.

"Oh," the realtor said flatly, her smile slipping, "you must be a local."

"Locals buy houses, don't they?"

"Of course they do. Sometimes. Usually not. Well, not here. They just leave." She tried to smile again, but instead pursed her lips. "You know, I'd appreciate if you didn't discuss that. California law doesn't require that kind of disclosure, and people die all the time, often in their homes. They have to die somewhere, don't they? And you know how superstitious people can be."

"You mean ghosts?"

"Well, the Chinese, but we don't get many Chinese people here. We do have a Thai restaurant near the airport though. The Hungry Lotus. Have you ever been? The service can be slow, but you can watch the planes land."

From behind him Stanley heard the grind of a large truck.

"Oh, my stagers. If you could just come back." She walked past him to the back of the truck where the doors opened, a ramp dropped down, and two unusually short, stout men in white jumpsuits started carrying down a paisley couch. They reminded him of oompa loompa men, the workers from the Willy Wonka movie, Lorna's favorite as a child, how they carried off all the naughty children. Back in his truck, Stanley headed to Main Street again, drove three more blocks and, turning again, was on another street much like Lorna's, lined with one-story bungalows. Wondering if this could be right, he glanced at the address he'd jotted down as he pulled up, this house farther back from the street, bordered by neatly trimmed hedges, a cement pathway leading to two glass doors, the kind stores or restaurants had, *Inyo County Coroner* stenciled discreetly on one, *Bishop Funeral Home* on the other. Not what he expected and only minutes from Lorna's, hiding in plain sight! If Lorna had only known. Stanley heard a knock at his window, and he jumped a little, a little girl on a bike looking in at him. He recognized her—she used to play with Dell—and rolled down the window. "Isabel, what are you doing over here?"

"Riding my bike, Mr. Stanley. I got it new for my birthday. Do you know when Dell's coming back? I want to show him."

"He had to move away. I'm sorry."

"But he didn't say goodbye."

"He told me to tell you goodbye."

"Is he coming back?"

"I don't know."

"What happened to your face?"

"I got hurt."

"Is this where you live, Mr. Stanley?" She took her hand off the handlebar and pointed toward the house.

"No, nobody lives there."

"I have to go now, Mr. Stanley. Bye."

He watched her ride down the street, handlebar streamers lifting up in the air. Then he looked over at the house again, two long driveways running along either side, curving around back. He rubbed his eyes. Caffeine was what he needed. Then he'd circle back. On Main Street again he pulled off into the first gas station. Inside, he poured a cup of coffee and went over to the register where the attendant, a man with a grizzled beard and thick glasses, waited. "Gas too?" the man asked.

"Just this, thanks." He pulled his wallet out and then looked past the man at the shelves of cigarettes and fishing gear, above them a piece of driftwood mounted on the wall. *I began to be sensible of strange feelings. I felt a melting in me. No more my splintered heart and maddened hand were turned against the wolfish world* was etched into it.

"What's that from?" Stanley asked.

"The big whale book. *Moby Dick*."

"You read it?" Stanley handed him a dollar.

"Well, it's a hard book to read. How about you? Looks like you tangled with a whale or two yourself."

"Bar room brawl. It's healing though."

"Where you headed?"

Stanley looked out to 395, almost forgetting he was in a tourist mecca, the Owens Valley, between the Sierras and the White Mountains. Other than to visit Lorna, he really hadn't spent much time in this area.

"The Ancient Bristlecone?" the man asked. "Death Valley? Or maybe you're a local. But then I'd know you."

"Locals go places too, don't they?"

The man chuckled. "Pardon me. I guess that was presumptuous." He put the money in the register. "Cream and sugar's over there."

"Just saw a house for sale a few streets over."

"Oh yeah, that one, where the lady died. A year ago, I think. With the boy. A real shame."

"How's that?"

"I guess it's a mystery, what happened to her."

"So you knew her?"

"The same way I know most people around here—yes, but not really. She came in with her boy once in a while like everyone else and bought things. Small lady, very pale. Pretty. Irish looking. Big eyes. Always looked a little scared or maybe worried. Her boy the same way, clinging to her leg."

"Scared, huh?"

"Yeah, like she lost something or might be lost. You know, when you first realize it but don't want to show it. Or maybe someone was after her. A deadbeat husband. The law. Who knows? There's enough of that around here. Why? You thinking of buying the place?"

"You said the Ancient Bristlecone is around here?"

"In the White Mountains, Route 168. Head down 395 to Big Pine. Great views. You'll see the sign. Visitor center burned down, but they're rebuilding it and the trees survived. 5000 years old. Old as Stonehenge. Can't kill them."

He'd heard about the place before, the ancient bristlecones up at 10,000 feet, the twisted trees, but had never made the trip up. "How's the road up?"

"Paved but it's not like Yosemite where all you have to do is pull off and you're on a trail. Here you have to drive deep *inside* a mountain to get anywhere. No armchair hikers here."

Back in his truck now, Stanley drove out of Bishop passing into Big Pine where he saw the Route 168 sign and turned left, ranchland and fences on both sides and up ahead another sign: Death Valley Road. No Services. Closed Due To Flooding. He'd heard about this backcountry way into the park to the Ubehebe Crater where the road out to the Racetrack Playa started, the place where the Fisher boy had disappeared. Passing it, he stayed on 168, well paved as the man said, taking him up into the desert scrub, up into the mountains, where another sign appeared: Bristlecone Visitors Center 25 miles. Stanley looked at his watch, knowing he should turn back, make the trip another time, and then in his rearview mirror at the road slipping away behind him. *The truth got you scared, huh?* Myra's voice came back to him.

He pressed the accelerator a little harder as the road steepened and got curvy, winding its way up inside the mountain, through steep canyon walls of scrub and wildflowers. Then, after another thousand feet, the road straightened and widened, and he slowed down, ahead a ranger booth, and stopping beside it he saw only crushed beer cans and candy wrappers inside it. Passing through, he pulled into a small gravel lot. He got out and walked across to a weathered picnic table and a park sign. Though still warm, it was windy here, and the terrain was a little different, still plenty of scrub but more trees now, slopes of pinyon pines and mountain mahogany, the tree types named on the sign in front of him. Standing there, he listened to the trees rustle as he peered at endless slopes of trees, one after another, forming a chain of shallow Vs, the road behind him quiet. Only thirteen miles from town, he could have been the only man left on earth, truth being you didn't have to go that far or be too far from a road to be alone. The world hadn't been completely ruined. A man could still walk off, he'd sometimes thought when doing mindless stuff like making up a room, and still disappear. That's what had happened the day the Fisher boy and his friends had left. Maidless, he'd made up the room himself. Rumpled blankets, bedspreads on the floor, wet towels piled in the bathroom, toothpaste smudged in the sink, nothing out of the usual. No tip either, but then he hadn't expected one—they were kids, upper-middle-class, he'd assumed. He glanced at his watch again and then over at the road behind him, still quiet, most tourists having already headed down to their motels or campers. Though there was still plenty of day left, he hadn't reached the ancient bristlecones yet, those higher up, he assumed, and it wasn't the sort of road you wanted to drive down in the dark. He looked down at the description of a short interpretive trail, nothing heavy duty and started along on it, a little rocky with a gentle upslope, just "an amble," the sign said. Here and there he stopped to scan more signs along the way, one in front of a patch of Mormon Tea, a shrub of shooting sprays, whorling up like flames.

> When food was scarce, Mormon settlers boiled the shrub's shoots, adding sugar, to lessen the bitterness. As the shrub was believed to be an effective treatment for syphilis, it was also called Whorehouse Tea.

Next came Utah Juniper, another shrub, with fragile, veil-like green foliage and purple berries. He plucked one and balanced it on his palm, the same palm on which the tiny white doll he'd so carefully carried up from the lightwell came to life. Junipers were hardy, according to the sign, some living 700 years, able to shoot root down fifty feet and spread it some 100 feet across. Even uprooted, juniper hibernated, some small part of them still living, ready to re-root. He kept walking, eventually circling around back to his truck. He got back in and continued up, the road eventually taking him outward, where the view opened up, ahead a sign for a lookout, and he pulled in. It was a stark, cold, even windier place with six parking spaces—in one, a beat-up convertible, a young couple in tie-dye T-shirts, bare feet up on the dashboard and in another, a van, its door slid open, revealing a family, grandparents and their grandkids, Stanley assumed. As he walked past, one of the kids, a little boy with a sandwich in his hand, waved to him, calling out, "Hey, mister," and the grandmother shushed him. Stanley lifted his hand, and then started climbing up the short, steep rocky trail.

At the top, he could see down into the Owens Valley, a patchwork of brown and green, green where the trees clustered around the towns and the open fields. It was dizzying, like looking down from an airplane, but here there was nothing to stop you from toppling, and humans, unlike junipers, broke easily, having no special way to re-root. Across the valley were the broad snowy shoulders of the Sierras, the various peaks one after another forming a long range. If only there were an easy way across, if he could walk on air. Turning, he headed back down to the lot. The van gone, the convertible was still there, the tie-dye couple in a clench now, kissing. He watched them for a moment, as if he had stumbled on two animals mating, and then got in his truck and backed out, continuing up another ten miles until he came to another sign: The Ancient Bristlecone Forest. In that lot were two orange Cal Trans trucks, one car, and three outhouses alongside the curb, and in the distance a fenced-off area from which he could hear saws and hammers, men inside the skeleton of what he assumed was the new visitor center. A lone rusted trailer, the make-shift visitor center, stood off to the left with a ramp leading up to it, but the door was shut. A sign outside it said Fee: $5.00. He put some money inside the box below it and walked over to the trailhead where there were a fork and trail descriptions: the one-mile Discovery Trail, exposed, steep, rocky, some trees shriveled, others stripped yellow and black, scarred by fire; or the four-mile Methuselah Trail, descending into the forest, named after the oldest bristlecone pine in the grove, 4700 years old, thousands of years older than Christ. Could he do that trail and make it back down to Bishop in time? But in time for what? He'd no idea whether Dr. LeBeau was even there. And he wasn't exactly acclimated. His heart would beat like a madman once he started upslope. Plus, after all of it he'd still need to get home, drive back to Bridgeport, and he wasn't supposed to be driving a lot in the first place. He looked back at the parking lot, at his truck, knowing what he should do. Or maybe if he quit procrastinating there'd be enough time to do the Methuselah and hightail it back down to Bishop before nightfall.

Stanley stepped into the shade of the forest, surprised to find sage up so high, and, leaning over, he pinched off a stalk, rubbed it between his fingers and held it to his nose, the aromatic scent reviving him. Everything would be all right. The trail, sloping gently downward, somehow made him think so, the forest closing round him, and as far as he could tell, he was alone, late-comers, if there were to be any, would probably opt for the shorter trail. Here and there he stopped at signs identifying a particular tree, ones far younger than the anonymous Methuselah, "unidentified for its own protection," the sign had said. It was a peaceful, shrouded place, the quiet pressed down, the hammering from the visitor center muffled by the rustling of the trees. He'd spent lots of time in lesser forests as a kid, if you could call them that, in the Sonora foothills where he and Lorna had played out great adventures, hiking deep in, hoping to become hopelessly lost, at least until they got hungry. Here among the bristlecones, a living graveyard, the oppressive weight of the dream, the tiny white doll, the bittersweet disappointment, had lifted slightly.

He sat down on a bench at an overlook and peered at a series of steep slopes, trees growing off their edges at crazy angles, cones and needles accumulating in the gullies. Some of the trunks were stout but battered-looking, striped black where lightning struck, yet their branches sprouted needles. He got up and walked to the trail's edge, looking down into a gully full of pinecones. He had the impulse to lie down, as he and Lorna had as children, and roll over the edge. There, in the gully, between walls, where his body would come to rest, he'd be protected, cocooned. Little would reach him there. He looked at his watch. *I understand grief, Mr. Uribe. I've lost people too.* Dr. Le Beau's voice came back to him again, but the pictures Sheriff Boyd had dropped off had formed their own images, telling him a story of oceans and sea creatures and men lashed to masts, hurled up in apocalyptic waves. How could he square that with the language of science, with what the autopsy report called "lesions of unknown origins," what he could be carrying around in his own heart? He might as well be struck by lightning; in fact, he didn't really care if he was. Or maybe he did. He stepped back onto the trail and kept walking, all upslope now, the trail having brought him down much lower than he'd realized only to bring him back up, circling around. But the light was starting to fade, the blue between the trees pale now. He was sweating a little. He picked up his pace, climbing up a steep switchback, before coming upon another bench, sitting on it two bearded old men.

"Well, what do you know, another homo sapien," one said, taking off his hat, a stocky, bald man in a plaid jacket.

"Hey, fellow," the other man said. Smaller and bony, he had a pointy beard and was wearing a black beret. He looked Stanley's way, but not directly at him. A pole rested between him and the other man. "We're the only ones left, come in at the end of trail to sit a bit, too late and too old to hike the whole trail."

"Yeah, the grim reaper creeping up on us," the stocky one said. "The living dead."

The smaller man placed his palm on the bench. "Still room for a third if you like." He looked out straight in front of him. He was blind, Stanley could see.

"Young men like him don't need rest," the stocky one said.

"Then what does he need?" the blind one asked.

The stocky one chuckled. "Hell if I know. Why don't you ask him?"

"I'm trying to get back to the parking lot," Stanley said. "You know how far it is?"

"Oh, you're already back," the blind one said. "No she-wolves here. *And a she-wolf, that with all hungerings/ Seemed to be laden in her meagreness,/ And many folk has caused to live forlorn!/ She brought upon me so much heaviness,/ With the affright that from her aspect came,/ That I the hope relinquished of the height.*"

"There he goes again, quoting Virgil," the stocky one said. "Don't mind him. He reads a lot."

"Dante. Virgil is the guide." The blind one turned his head back toward Stanley. "You've come full circle, young man. The visitor center isn't far off. Just behind us. The crew quit a little while ago."

"Thanks," Stanley said, passing behind the men.

"Anything for mankind," the blind one said.

"Mankind my ass," the stocky one said.

Up ahead Stanley saw a fork and then five minutes later through the trees the visitor center. Coming around it, he stepped onto pavement and saw the parking lot, only his truck in it now. Though the sun was starting to set, it was far from dark, but Stanley switched on his headlights anyway given how exposed and narrow the road was, and started heading down, passing the lookout, the lot empty now, the tie-dye couple gone. As he continued his descent, he kept checking his rearview mirror for the old men from the bench. No campgrounds close by, he'd no idea where they'd come from or how they'd get back, but then again they'd probably just chuckle at his concern, his foolishness, the utter waste of youth. Passing through the unmanned ranger booth, he glanced at his watch, thinking he was too late. Entering the winding canyon, he tightened his grip on the wheel as he kept descending, the darkening walls of desert scrub closing in on him. His tires screeched a little and then slipped off the edge, but he pulled the truck back up and then suddenly shot out into the straightaway. He was making good time, but he could see down below in the distance plenty of rush hour traffic. He didn't see how he could make it, Dr. LeBeau likely having left for the day if he was ever there at all. And he still had a long drive back home where an unhappy Sheriff Boyd would probably eventually show up.

At the 395 intersection, waiting to turn in, he watched the traffic, cars and campers, some with bikes on the back, and long trucks slowly pass, dark enough now that he could see headlights and brake lights. Then space opened, and he entered the flow, lit-up billboards rising from the ranchland like giant movie screens: YOU ARE NOT ALONE, above a picture of a pregnant girl cradling her belly, Life Is Profound Foundation or LIP. SAY NO TO DRUGS. THIS WAY YOU'LL HAVE MORE TIME TO DRINK! A six pack of beer. SAVE THE DATE!

CHRIST ON THE REBOUND! A pad and pen. GET BACK YOUR LIFE. FREE BARIATRIC SURGERY MEETINGS. A doctor in a white gown standing over a patient on a gurney.

Stanley felt a gnawing in his stomach, coffee the only thing he'd had all day. The golden arches were rising in the distance—a McDonald's billboard—and then another one, a rippling red line of EKG peaks and valleys: JESUS IN A HEARTBEAT. Then a golf course, sprinklers watering it. STRESSED OUT? TRY A ROUND IN PARADISE! Then, finally, the single lane opened to two lanes, everything speeding up, and soon he crossed into the outskirts of Bishop. Ahead though he could see more congestion, but he got lucky, making all the lights, passing through town, back where he was supposed to be, wait-ing to turn, like any man, off from work, heading home for a warm dinner. And after he turned, feeling the wheel slipping through his hands, he found himself in front of Dr. LeBeau's office again with the two glass doors. Sliding down a little in his seat, he closed his eyes, listening to the hum of distant traffic. He crossed his arms and tried to rest for a few minutes, even though he knew his time was running out. He heard a sharp knock at his window and saw a man this time, dark liquid eyes topped with a thick swatch of brow, a mustache, a head of hair.

"Mr. Uribe? Is that you?"

Stanley rolled down his window. "Am I too late?"

"No. Please." The doctor straightened up and stepped back. Stanley got out and followed him up the walkway. As the doctor unlocked the door, Stanley felt something brush against his leg and heard a meow.

The doctor laughed softly. "Our neighborhood stray." Then he pushed the door open.

Inside now Stanley stood in a small waiting room, two chairs and the usual coffee table magazine spread. "If you could wait here," the doctor said, and then walked through another door, closing it part way.

Sitting down, Stanley picked up a magazine, *Outdoor Explo-rations*, on its cover a man's wind-burnt face, hood scrunched around it. He opened up to a snow-covered mountain. *One of the worst avalanches in history,* red Xs marking the buried bodies. He flipped a few pages to a hammerhead shark gliding through a reef. *Electroreceptors in the shark's body allow them to detect the electrical activity of their prey, even the heartbeat of fish buried under the ocean floor. No one yet knows how evolution brought this about.*

"Please come in, Mr. Uribe." The door wide open now, the doctor gestured to a chair inside and then sat behind his desk, a large wooden one with stacks of files on it. "Interesting, isn't it, the Everest story, the top of the world."

Stanley looked down, surprised the magazine was still in his hand. He started to get up, but the doctor raised his hand. "That can wait, Mr. Uribe. Please. Sit." He gestured to the chair again. "Sheriff Boyd told me about your accident. Said you were very lucky. Your sister, on the other hand, was very, very unlucky." The doctor opened a folder.

Stanley recognized the image, even upside down—the man on the wave clinging to the mast.

"I take it Sheriff Boyd gave you these pictures, cross sections of your sister's heart. I don't know what he said, but they show something I've never seen before—these sorts of lesions all over your sister's heart." He turned the image around. "This one," he pointed down to part of the image, "is in a particularly dangerous place, near the AV node, the pathway where electricity travels, making the heart beat. I believe it was this lesion that blocked the pathway, resulting in a fatal arrhythmia. Given its location, I'm surprised your sister lived as long as she did. In some ways actually she was very lucky."

"Lucky? Lucky is living to a 100," Stanley said, suddenly angry, even though he knew very well from his time at *The Sonora* that longevity wasn't always lucky.

"Now the key issue here is the origin of the lesions, whether they're congenital or genetic, the result of a defective gene or genes inherited from one or both of your parents."

"And if it's congenital?"

"It means the lesions are unique to her and likely started growing at or shortly after birth and are no threat to you or her son. But if it's genetic, that means both of you could carry that gene or genes and be at risk. Has anyone else in your family died unexpectedly?"

Stanley shrugged. "An uncle, on my father's side, maybe. A sheepherder. Supposedly he drowned in a pond, even though he could swim."

"Was there an autopsy?"

"I was a kid then, and there's no one left to ask. My father has Alzheimer's. Can't you test for the gene?"

"We'd have no idea which gene to look for. We could biopsy your heart to see if you have any lesions, but that's a very dangerous procedure on the living."

Stanley sighed, felt himself getting mad all over again. He rubbed the back of his neck. "So why bother telling me? I mean what am I supposed to do now?"

"Sometimes there are symptoms. Lightheadedness. Fainting. Potential precursors to a fatal event. But often there aren't. Often death is the first symptom. I wish I could be more definitive. I know how frustrating this must be. Your sister. The long wait. But I think it's better to know than not know, and Sheriff Boyd said you wanted to know. In the future, though, these genes may be identified and tested for."

"And then what?"

"A defibrillator, a small device can be implanted under the skin, to shock your heart back into rhythm. Or maybe in the distant future gene therapy."

"If I don't drop dead before then."

"Or it may be you're perfectly healthy. You don't carry the gene at all, or even if you do it may never get triggered. You see we probably all carry defective genes, but that doesn't mean they're going to make us sick or kill us. No one really knows yet, though one day we probably will."

"It still doesn't make sense. All the times Lorna went to the doctor, and the doctors said it was all in her head, all her illnesses. And now you're telling me she was *right*?" Stanley felt the anger welling up again, but he knew it was no use. He thought of his angels gliding back and forth beneath the unchanging light, the cheerful oompa loompa men chanting their morbid jingles.

"I examined your sister's medical records. Despite all her doctor visits she never had an EKG, which is unfortunate. If she had, they might have picked up on it, but then again an EKG is only a snapshot, a brief portrait of the heart's rhythm. Even a damaged heart can beat normally for a time and then suddenly go haywire. Diagnosing a condition for which there's no name, no precedent, in an asymptomatic patient isn't easy, Mr. Uribe. I wouldn't blame the doctors, and of course your sister had OCD, complicating matters."

"Would she have known?"

"Known? No, I don't think so. She would have lost consciousness quickly. She didn't suffer. She was in her pajamas. She looked asleep. Her body was immaculate."

"Immaculate?"

"Yes, immaculate."

"So what am I supposed to do?"

"I recommend a full cardiac work up—EKG, echocardiogram, stress test—if for nothing else but peace of mind. I recommended the same for her son. Any cardiologist can do this. If all come back normal, then you should live your life." The doctor rose.

"Then that's it?"

"I'm sorry. I wish there were more. I'll mail the final autopsy report once it's done." The doctor walked around the desk and took the magazine from Stanley. "Thank you for coming in, Mr. Uribe, and please accept my condolences." He walked him out to the front door.

Stanley stood outside now. It was nearly dark and chilly. The smell of cooked food hung in the air. And the cat was back, at his feet again, its iridescent eyes peering up at him. He started down the walkway, assuming the cat would stop short at the sidewalk, but it followed him to the truck, and as he opened the door the cat jumped in, gingerly stepping across to the passenger seat. Stanley looked back at the coroner's office. Dark now, it looked like nobody was home. Stanley got in the truck and looked over at the cat. He'd never had one, and he recalled a motel guest, an old man telling him how after his wife had died, he'd come home from the hospital only to find a cat at his door. "And I've been a slave to it ever since," he'd said. Stanley reached over and lightly stroked the cat's head, and the cat, closing its eyes, started purring. Then, lights on, he headed back up to Main Street where the traffic had thinned out. He rubbed his eyes, the bones around them aching now. He remembered Caitlin's warning about concussions. Ahead was a blinking neon sign, Pablo's Cantina, a red sombrero and green cactus on it, a place he'd been to before with Lorna and Dell, but he let it pass and glanced over at the cat, curled up now nose to tail. Sleep— just what he needed. Then he could sort things out. Ahead were more bright signs, motel alley, one with a giant lit-up bristlecone on it—The Ancient Bristlecone Lodge & Suites, a place like his with a creek, except here the creek ran right through the motel courtyard. He'd always wanted to see it. He turned, pulling into a semi-circle. As he got out, the cat lifted its head, blinking at him. At the entrance, sliding glass doors parted, and he stepped into a spacious cedar-planked lobby, large colorful photographs of the Sierras from the gallery down the street, he assumed, and plush, upholstered chairs encircling a brick fireplace. On the other side was an eating area with tables and a long counter to slide trays and large glass jugs with silver spigots of water, iced tea, and lemonade alongside a large platter of cookies, freshly baked, he assumed, since the whole lobby smelled of warm sugar, a far cry from his Mr. Coffee Maker and Styrofoam cups and oily Danish. No deer heads either.

"Welcome to the Ancient Bristlecone. How can we help you, sir?" The clerk, a young woman with a blond ponytail, smiled. A nametag—Annette—was pinned to her blouse.

"Any rooms for tonight?"

"How many in your party, sir?"

Stanley glanced back at his truck. "Just me."

"How many nights?"

"One."

"Mountainside or Creekside? Creekside's more expensive, but quieter. I have one left in the back. Two queen beds. $129.99 per night."

Stanley pulled out his wallet and handed her a credit card, even though it was double his rate for his best room.

She pulled out a motel map. "Pull around the back and park right there. Pool closes at ten p.m. Breakfast is from seven until ten a.m. Check out is at eleven. No pets." She handed him his room key. "And, oh, please don't feed the ducks. Enjoy your stay."

In his truck again, Stanley drove around back where it was much darker, the only light from lot-facing rooms and a neon sign flashing Bishop Bowl next door. He pulled his keys out of the ignition and looked over at the cat. He'd never picked one up before, much less smuggled one into a motel. He walked around to the other side and opened the door. Leaning in, he gently slid his hand under the cat's belly and slowly pulled it toward him. To his surprise, the cat went limp, and as he held him against his chest, he thought he could feel its heart beating.

Inside now, he avoided the elevator, taking the stairs up instead, steep and carpeted, burgundy with a whimsical goldfish pattern. After hurrying down the hallway past more wildlife photographs, he swiped his card key and pushed the door open. Inside, he let the cat down on a bed and then went back and hung the Do Not Disturb sign outside the door. Then he went over and sat on the other bed, exhausted. Still, he wouldn't sleep. Not yet. It had been a long time since he'd been a motel guest, and working in the business, he didn't know if he could enjoy it, knowing how difficult even pleasant people could be, how dirty even a cleaned room could be, but then again this was no hole in the wall. Even the cat, curled up against a pillow, seemed to know it, and now that he got a better look at the animal he thought it was surprisingly healthy looking, not scrawny at all, its thick fur dark brindled, its tail ringed and notched at the end. True, he'd violated motel policy, smuggling it in, but it was just for a night and plenty of his guests had done the same, leaving behind all sorts of critters, usually cold-blooded things—iguanas, snakes, even a baby alligator swimming in the bathtub. Shifting his gaze now, he let his eyes roam from the dark-brown wallpaper, its texture mimicking wood grain, walnut furniture, and brass sconces framing the headboards to the smooth, popcorn-free ceiling and the wood-planked floors, not real wood, but some sort of composite. All very clever. Stanley lay back on his bed, letting his head sink into the pillow, but then he sat back up. Wait. Cody. Tomorrow was his day off, but he'd need him to open in the morning. As he reached for the phone, it suddenly rang, startling him. He stared at it, letting it ring a few more times and then picked it up.

"Mr. Uribe, it's Annette from the front desk to see if you need anything."

"Need?"

"To make your stay more pleasant."

It had never even occurred to him to make such a call, to head off a complaint from the get-go, but then again his rooms were dumpy. God knows what he'd have to go through. "I'm fine. Thank you." He got up and went over to the sliding door stepping out onto the balcony. He sat down in a chair—two on either side of a small glass table—and looked down at the creek. It was running fast through the flagstone courtyard, swaths of fat orange marigolds blanketing its banks, above it, a blue pool, all lit by ornate candelabras. All the courtyard rooms had a view like this, a much better set-up than his own place where you had to hike down behind the motel into the bramble to get a glimpse of the river.

It was getting dark when they pulled off I-5 again, in Santa Nella, into a crowded lot near a Bavarian-style building with a giant rotating windmill attached to it. Beside it was a run-down motel, The Happy Valley Inn. Last year it was something else; Grace couldn't remember what. This was their last rest stop before nightfall and the endless monotony, headlights briefly lighting up pieces of farmland and shadowy figures inside passing cars. It always spooked Grace, driving I-5 at night. She slipped on a sweater. Then she and Elwood walked into the building, on one side an open-air store: cans of Janssen Pea Soup stacked in a pyramid, small gunny sacks of split peas piled in wooden barrels, jars of pea jelly, sets of miniature utensils—fork, knife, spoon—and shelves of coffee mugs and dangling glove mitts all with the cartoonish, pot-bellied, winking chef in a giant chef's hat on it, Janssen's logo. On the other side was the restaurant where they always ate on the way home.

"Welcome to Janssen Pea," the hostess at the lectern said. She wore an ankle-length dress covered by a gingham apron, and her hair was rolled up in a tight bun. She looked Mormon or Mennonite, though Grace doubted she was either. Pulling menus, the hostess led them to a booth.

Grace slid in, the leather seat on her side torn, covered with electrical tape, and made a quick survey of the white walls and dark wood molding, faux spider plants tumbling down from wall-mounted boxes. Same as last year. Across the aisle a bus boy was clearing off plates of half-eaten food and sliding them into a plastic tub. Then he swept more food out from under the table.

"Why don't you get what you got last time—the shrimp?" Elwood said. "Wasn't that good?"

Grace flipped through the menu, its plastic pages sticky. She wiped her hands with a napkin.

"Well," Elwood chuckled, "it's not the Inn."

"The food wasn't great there either, just all dressed up and overpriced. The date bread was good though. Can you order that for me, the shrimp? I'm going to the restroom." Grace slid out. Walking through the store area, she gazed at the knick-knacks, the stuffed animals, polka-dotted flip-flops, refrigerator magnets, baby dolls, and endless wood-mounted wall hangings—"Don't just count your blessings. Share them." "Despair is the enemy of happiness." "God will keep you." And a wall of books—*Why Men Have Fallen to Pieces; You Are as Good as You Think; I Love You, Do You Love Me?*

In the restroom now, she walked down a short hallway. At the end of it was a full-length mirror, around it girls in shorts and sandals smirking and frowning, fastening and unfastening their hair. And above the mirror another sign: "Integrity is how you live your life when no one's looking." In fact, Grace, scanning the whole restroom, saw sayings everywhere. "If tears could build a stairway, I'd walk up to heaven and bring you home." "A heart without a home is no home." "Eternity is an endless chain of nows." "The meaning of life is to give life meaning." "Don't be afraid to go out on a limb where the fruit is." Grace shut the stall door and locked it, thankful nothing was staring back at her. She opened her purse and pulled out the flyer of the ancient, mud-chipped boy, and suddenly realized where she'd seen that face before—at home in a newspaper article about the terra cotta warriors, an army of them discovered underground in China scheduled to arrive at San Francisco's Asian Art Museum. But it didn't make sense, one warrior having dropped out of the plane, lost in some cornfield? She stepped out of the stall, washed her hands, and then went back to the table, but Elwood was gone. She looked around. She was at the right one, wasn't she? She looked down at the cushion, the electrical tape over the tear, and slid in. The waitress, carrying a tray, stopped at the table and unloaded their drinks, a basket of rolls, and two salads. "It comes with the meal," she said.

"Have you seen my husband? He was sitting right here."

The waitress flipped through her order pad. "Let's see. Table ten. A burger and the shrimp, right?" Tapping her pen on the pad, she peered down the aisle toward the entrance and then, turning, surveyed the room. "Probably went to the restroom. Want me to get the manager?"

Grace shook her head. "He's probably just looking around the store."

"Well, there's a lot to see. Enough junk for a lifetime."

Grace spread her napkin on her lap. She took a roll out of the basket and tore a piece off. It was warm and doughy and smelled of yeast. Looking down the aisle to the entrance, she saw the aproned hostess armed with menus, leading a family of four down the aisle, and thought maybe he'd gone back to the car, forgotten something there, and then a movie scene flashed in her mind, a gas station in the rainy mountains of the Puget Sound where a couple stops on their way home, the woman carrying out two steaming cups of coffee only to find her husband gone, his seat empty, a long flatbed hauling logs pulling out. Grace put the other half of the roll back in the basket and then started to slide out of the booth again, but then Elwood was coming down the aisle.

"That bad?" he asked, sliding in.

Grace looked down at her salad, at the sallow tomatoes and croutons on yellow iceberg lettuce. She picked up her fork. "It comes with the meal."

"Good." Elwood picked up his napkin and spread it on his lap. "Something wrong?"

Grace put down her fork and pulled the flyer out of her bag and pushed it toward him. "It was in the women's restroom at the other rest stop, taped to the stall door."

"What is it?"

"A missing warrior. Life-size terra cotta soldiers found in a tomb in China. There's an exhibit in the city. I read about it in the newspaper."

Elwood pushed the flyer back to her.

"See what it says and the phone number on it. All those flyers of missing children, real ones, and then this. Isn't that weird?"

Elwood looked down at the flyer again. "'2,312 years old and muddy?' I don't see how anyone could think that's a real person. It's probably just some kind of marketing scheme."

"In poor taste, posting it there, don't you think?"

"With a pointed hood and body armor?"

"Well, I'm going to call them up."

Elwood picked up his fork and started eating his salad.

"Where were you anyway?"

"Same place as you."

"All those sayings in the restroom? Is that what kept you so long?"

"What?"

"You know—Home Is Where the House Is."

"You're not the only one that has the right to disappear, Grace."

Grace folded the flyer back up and put it in her bag. "I didn't want to wake you."

"You weren't really on a walk, were you?"

"Well, I was. At Salt Creek. You're always in such a rush to leave I didn't think you'd want to stop. There were horseflies. Just like Jared said. And I found the mallard too, but I had to get off the boardwalk, follow a trail out."

"By yourself?"

"I didn't have to go far. We can go back together. Next year."

"Well, I went into the store and bought something."

"Not one of those sayings."

He pulled out a black velvet box and opened it. "Two dollars. Hope you won't make me get down on my knee for it."

Their waitress put down dinner plates. "Oh, so you're back. The runaway husband." She chuckled.

"We're getting married," Elwood said.

The waitress looked down at the ring. "Need any refills?"

Elwood shook his head. "I think we have everything."

8

Cocooned in the warm darkness, Stanley kept his eyes shut, not wanting to wake up, but a zipper was coming down, light pouring in, Dr. LeBeau's voice—*I understand grief, Mr. Uribe. I've lost people too*, and then pin pricks on his chest, and suddenly he thrust himself up, his heart pounding as the cat sprang off him, yowling. Stanley looked over at the sliding glass door—he'd never shut the curtain—and, shielding his eyes, looked at the cat, which was crouched at the foot of the bed now warily eyeing him. "Sorry, Bishop." The name just slipped out. He glanced at the clock. He was hungry. The cat probably was too. Breakfast almost over, he quickly got dressed and went down the hallway where he saw a cleaning woman beside a towel cart. "Morning."

"*Buenos días, señor.*"

He pointed down the hallway toward his room. "*No es necesario* to clean room 224. *Dos veintecuatro.*" He couldn't remember how to say two hundred.

The woman looked at her clipboard. "Okay, *señor*. 224. You check out today?"

"*Sí. Gracious.*" He headed toward the elevator, pausing there at an overlook, below, the breakfast room, people lined up, pushing trays along the food bar, the smell of bacon and coffee drawing him down. Passing the front desk, Stanley picked up a newspaper and then, getting in line, put a warm plate and silverware on his tray. The place was noisy with clanking silverware and chattering guests. Eggs, sausage, oatmeal, cold cereals, fresh melon, cranberry and orange juice, it was quite a spread, even a waffle maker, dripping with batter, a little boy and girl transfixed, as their batter plumped up. Hot breakfast, the recent trend in the motel industry, was impossible at his place, and besides most people didn't stick around long enough, anxious

to get where they were going, a better place, and more than a
hot breakfast would be needed to change that. After filling his
plate, he got some milk and juice, and then sat down at the
only vacant table, front-facing, looking out to Main Street. A
long time since he'd had a breakfast made for him, he ate some
egg and took a sip of juice and then looked around the room.
He was the only one eating solo, but everyone else was too
busy nagging their kids or reading tourist books to notice. Or
maybe they'd assumed him married, a late sleeper, wife having
already fed the kids, or single, his buddies too hungover to eat.
Or maybe he was simply himself, a man separated from his wife
with a nearby motel whose kid sister had died suddenly of an
unknown disease, a possible death card in his back pocket, and
a cat named Bishop hidden in his room. He looked down at his
tray, at the glass of frothy milk he'd gotten for the cat, and then
ate some bacon and started leafing through the newspaper.
"Fire Burns Close to Yosemite" "Flesh Eating MRSA on the
Rise" "Diplomacy Shifts the Focus." He turned the page again,
his eye landing on a series of mini stories.

NEWLYWED DEATH IN CANYONLANDS

> Married for only a week, Emily Castle, 30, admitted to
> pushing her husband Nate Fletcher, 35, to his death off
> a cliff at Canyonlands National Park in Moab, Utah.
> Castle, who first denied being with Fletcher when he
> fell, later admitted they'd had a fight, and when she
> tried to leave, Fletcher tried to pull her back, and she
> pushed him. Castle's friends reported that the couple
> had always had a rocky relationship, Castle calling the
> wedding off more than once. But, according to Fletch-
> er's friend Elliot Wiley, "Nate couldn't wait to start a
> family, to have kids. He adored her. He couldn't live
> without her. I can't believe she did this on purpose."
> Sentencing is scheduled for next month.

Stanley looked up. An old couple carrying trays was coming
his way. All the tables full, Stanley started to rise, but the old

man said, "No rush, son. We can wait."

The old woman put her tray down on the table and smiled. "Or share."

Stanley sat back down.

"That bad, eh?" The old man, after sitting down, looked over at Stanley's plate. "Our first night here."

Stanley looked at his plate—too much piled on—and gestured to his newspaper. "I was just—"

"You see that one about the man dead in his car for a week?" the old man said. "Behind the wheel."

The old woman tore a packet of sugar and poured it in her coffee and sighed. "Poor fellow. Everyone must have thought he was sleeping."

"In midtown Manhattan? What kind of world is this?" The old man reached for the saltshaker and salted his eggs.

"The kind where you let people eat in peace," the old woman said, chuckling.

The old man laughed and beamed at his wife. "Eighty-eight years old today and still beautiful, isn't she? That's why we're here—to celebrate. Her parents lived past 100. Can you believe that?"

"They were tailors for Saks Fifth Avenue in Manhattan. That's where we're from, but we live in Pasadena now," the old woman said. "My mother had terrible asthma but could still thread a needle at ninety-nine."

"Her father was senile though," the old man said, "wandered the streets of New York, in and out of markets stuffing his pockets with Brach candies."

"Sometimes he'd come home bruised," the old woman continued. "We never knew if he fell or got beat up, and he couldn't remember. But what about you?"

"Fisherman? Hunter? Hiker?" the old man asked.

"Neither actually. Just passing through and checking out today."

"That's too bad," the old woman said.

Stanley pushed his chair back and started to stand up.

"Oh, we didn't mean to chase you away," the old woman said.

"That's right," the old man said. "Sit. Finish."

"Thanks, but I've had my fill." Stanley started to lift his tray.

"Your newspaper." The old woman slid it on his tray and then, reaching into her bag, pulled out a piece of paper and folded it in half. "And this too." She put it on top of the newspaper.

Sighing, the old man shook his head. "She gives those to everyone."

"No, not everyone," the old woman said.

After Stanley bused his tray, he went back to his room. Sitting down on the bed, he put the milk on the nightstand, and the cat, eyes wide, suddenly got up and started lapping at it. Then Stanley laid the newspaper on the bed and unfolded the piece of paper.

The Journey
By James Wright

Anghiari is medieval, a sleeve sloping down
A steep hill, suddenly sweeping out
To the edge of a cliff, and dwindling.
But far up the mountain, behind the town,
We too were swept out, out by the wind,
Alone with the Tuscan grass.

Wind had been blowing across the hills
For days, and everything now was graying gold
With dust, everything we saw, even
Some small children scampering along a road,
Twittering Italian to a small caged bird.
We sat beside them to rest in some brushwood,
And I leaned down to rinse the dust from my face.

I found the spider web there, whose hinges
Reeled heavily and crazily with the dust,

Whole mounds and cemeteries of it, sagging
And scattering shadows among shells and wings.
And then she stepped into the center of air
Slender and fastidious, the golden hair
Of daylight along her shoulders, she poised there,
While ruins crumbled on every side of her.
Free of the dust, as though a moment before
She had stepped inside the earth, to bathe herself.

I gazed, close to her, till at last she stepped
Away in her own good time.

Many men
Have searched all over Tuscany and never found
What I have found there, the heart of the light
Itself shelled and leaved, balancing
On filaments themselves falling. The secret
Of this journey is to let the wind
Blow its dust all over your body,
To let it go on blowing, to step lightly, lightly
All the way through your ruins, and not to lose
Any sleep over the dead, who surely
Will bury their own, don't worry.

He looked over at the door, at the peephole, half expecting the old couple to be on the other side, wondering what
he thought of it, and then he looked over at the cat, its pink
tongue darting in and out, milk dribbling over the edge. Then
he noticed the phone, its red light blinking. Had the maid come
in anyway? Or maybe it was just another courtesy call, a polite
check-out reminder. He understood the pressure, especially in
a motel that pulled in crowds like this, getting rooms cleaned
before guests returned for the day or a new wave checked in.
Still, he had a little time. He lifted the receiver and pulled up the
message, but it was only a hang-up. Taking the newspaper, he
stepped out onto the balcony. Now in the full light of day he
marveled at the marigolds again—he'd never seen so many—

hundreds of them all over the creek's banks, fat and orange, so bright they didn't even seem real, and then the quiet blue pool, a green hose snaking down into it, a worker kneeling at the edge. Shifting his eye back to the creek, to a calm pond right below him where the creek bulged out, he saw a trio of ducks resting in a circle, chattering to each other, and then he looked at the creek again rolling swiftly toward the front of the motel, disappearing under Main Street. Sitting down, he opened the newspaper.

NEW CHANCE AT SIGHT

Yenay Yang, a six-year-old girl, was the victim of a disturbing attack in a remote province of China. Lured into a corn field by an elderly man offering her drug-laced sweets, Yenay was found hours later bloodied and crying by a farmer who rushed her to a local hospital where doctors discovered her eyes had been cut out. Authorities believe she fell prey to a growing black market for organs. The lucrative trade isn't always money driven or highly organized though. The attacker could have been a solo operator in desperate need of corneas for himself or a loved one going blind. Yenay, flown to Kern Children's Hospital near Los Angeles, is scheduled to undergo experimental surgery in an attempt to restore some of her sight. Yenay's mother said, "She keeps asking when morning will come."

Wondering what the old man would have thought of that, Stanley went back into the room, to the bed where the cat was now sitting, licking its paw, and then picked up the poem again.

I found the spider web there, whose hinges
Reeled heavily and crazily with the dust,
Whole mounds and cemeteries of it, sagging.

Then he looked over at the clock. Almost out of time he got into the shower, a spacious enclosure with a glass door. No stained grout or musty smell. No ceiling mold. Plenty of towels. God, he could live here forever. True, Cody would be upset, disappointed in him, ditching his life. Caitlin would be worried sick and then write him off. And what about his father? Soon he wouldn't know any different. Lathering and rinsing, he let the hot water pelt him. But no doubt Sheriff Boyd would find him, lecturing him on cowardice. Then, toweled off, he put his clothes on and went back in the room and, pulling a twenty from his wallet, dropped it on the pillow along with his room key. Then, he picked up the cat and headed out the door, down the steps to his truck. Cat on the passenger seat, Stanley started to back out but stopped short. The Do Not Disturb sign. Trying to remember if he'd pulled it off, he looked over at the cat, but the cat, sunk down, sphinxlike, just gazed out the windshield. The maid would eventually go in anyway, he knew, but still he got out and ran back up. His room door though was already propped open, so he started backing away as the maid came rushing out. "Oh, *señor*, your wallet." She held it out to him.

Stanley reached behind to his back pocket. Had it dropped out in the bathroom? He took the wallet and pulled out the rest of his money and held it out to her.

"Oh no, *señor*." She stepped back and pulled from her smock the twenty he'd left her. "*No es necesario. Gracious.*"

But Stanley, having dropped all his cash, was already heading down the steps. Out the door, he went back to his truck and drove out of the lot onto Main Street. He put on his sunglasses and glanced over at the cat. Curled up now, it was sleeping. Approaching the outskirts of town, Stanley saw open space, scrub and arid mountains ahead, and then as Main Street turned into 395 the road started pitching up, trees and forest, in the distance thunderheads hanging low. Mammoth Lakes next, he thought maybe he should pull off and pick up a litter box, cat food, but then again he'd just given all his money away. He took off his sunglasses, a dark cloud blocking the sun now. A large raindrop hit his windshield and then a few more. He turned on the wipers. Then the sky unloaded, the rain pounding his windshield, blocking his view. The cat, lifting its head, looked over at Stanley and blinked. "Don't worry, Bishop," Stanley said, slowing down, keeping his eyes on what he could see of the yellow line until the rain eased and he was suddenly out of it, past Mammoth and heading toward Mono Lake, back suddenly in the sun. That's how it was up here—you could just as fast drive into a thing as out of it. He put his sunglasses back on and turned off the wipers, the windshield streaked with water. Ahead was Mono Lake and then the sign for Navy Beach. Turning, he headed down a narrow gravel road, puddled here and there from the rain. Men, heading to the gallows, walked around puddles, he'd heard. He went slow, walled in by tall scrub, wary of another car coming up the other way. Ahead was the parking lot, and soon he saw the blue-green shore, the gentle surge of the water, the tufa rising up, and in the distance the other smaller islands, one of them where the gulls gave birth, where the Madison boy's bones had been found. He pulled into a spot.

Across the lake, too far away to see, was the boardwalk, where Myra probably was now, binoculars trained on the lake, maybe even on him, and above it, Lorna. If he'd only believed her. The tree scratching at her window, boogeyman in the closet—at first it was the usual kid stuff, but then the brain tumor, a glioblastoma. What kid asks about such things? *Are you sure, Stanley? Are you sure it's not there? Feel again, Stanley.* And from then on it never stopped, the only thing that ever reassured her, gave her solace, albeit briefly, was some stupid psychic at a wedding she'd gone to, turning over cards in a tent, saying she'd live into her nineties. He looked over at the cat. Awake now, it was tracking a small spider scuttling across the seat, the spider stopping and starting until finally the cat, lifting its paw, flattened it and then ate it.

Stanley cracked the window and got out. The beach was empty, except for a family of four, their backs to him, in bathing suits sitting on a blanket. Beyond them, way out in the lake, were flocks of gulls and phalaropes, bulking up on shrimp brine. That's what the lake was, a rest area for migrating birds, the islands, a nursery for expecting mothers. Most of California's gulls were born here. Mark Twain called this place the Dead Sea, but it was anything but dead, despite it being three times as salty as the ocean. All this he'd learned from Myra on his boardwalk visits. Having walked past the family down the beach, he stood at the water's edge, where tiny black flies sprung up in a dark cloud around his feet and landed again, brimming the lake. Off to his left gulls were running along the shoreline, mouths open, feasting on the flies. Stepping back a little, Stanley took off his clothes, stripping down to his underwear, dropping his keys and wallet on top. He glanced back at the family and then walked through the dark band of flies. They didn't bite; he hardly felt them at all and saw ribbons of tiny shrimp floating across the water. He'd never actually gone fully into the lake. Few people did. Perhaps they thought it was illegal, but California no longer used it for drinking water, so no ranger was going to pull him out, cite him. He was simply a man going for an early-season swim.

He stepped into the water. It was cool but not cold. He didn't shudder or shrink from it. His toes didn't cramp. It only seemed odd that he'd never gone fully in before. He took a few more steps forward, the bottom rocky in spots, the water getting deeper. Life started in water; maybe it should end there too. But then he remembered again how Lorna, just born, swaddled in the hospital nursery, had beat the air with her tiny red fists, how she was probably beating them now against the lid of her coffin, screaming *No. Go back!* as he inched toward some hidden precipice, some drop-off, where the ground would slip out beneath him, and he'd be sucked into deep water. But to drown here, you'd have to hold yourself down or be held down, the water so salty, unlike Lake Tahoe, where the cold water brought its dead down, held them there, preserved. Stanley looked back again at the family on the beach and then took several more steps until he was waist high, only his chest exposed. Arms stretched out, he fell backward, the way kids did, expecting to be caught. He didn't sink; the water held him as it lapped around his face, swirled in his ears, and he finally felt the pleasant sensation of floating, of being carried. The water would take him where it would, and it wouldn't matter. Peering up at the sky, he watched a flock of birds swooping, bank left, then right, each bird impossibly close to another. He thought of an old movie Lorna once described about two elderly sisters, once child actors, living out their days in a rotting Hollywood mansion, one sister paralyzed, the other, a crazy drunk who kills her sister's beloved parakeet, serving it up to her on a bed of tomatoes. "That's how we're going to end up," Lorna had joked. "I'll be the crazy one." And then there was Rusty, the drunk he'd bought the motel from, who'd plowed into the woman, leaving her to die—or had he made that up, wanting to be worse than he was?

Stanley turned his head, thinking he'd floated out a ways toward the center, to the deep water, too far out to get back, but he wasn't far from where he'd started. He pulled himself back up to his feet and trudged toward the shore and out of the water. After pulling on his pants, he grabbed his shirt, keys, wallet, and headed up the beach. He could see that they were all watching him, that family—the parents and their two children, a girl and a boy—and he felt foolish knowing they'd seen him half naked. Running his tongue over his lips, he tasted the bitter salt of the lake as he approached the family. There on the blanket on the white sand in their bathing suits they were a pretty picture, the mother in a red bathing suit, her long pale legs folded up beneath her, the father, with a chest of dark hair, the little boy fair like the mother, the girl, doe-eyed and delicate. European, he assumed. Myra said the Americans, too horrible in bathing suits, never sat on this beach. The mother was talking. "You see, people travel the world to take in the waters," but the little boy, cutting her off, pointed at Stanley. "Look, Mama. A ghost." The mother smiled over at Stanley apologetically, and then turned to the boy, putting her finger to her mouth. "Shh. That's not a nice thing to say."

Stanley looked at his chest and his arms, already dry, covered in a white powder, a fine veil of salt, but his hair, still wet, dripped, burning his eyes.

"But, Mama," the little girl said, "why is the ghost crying?"

"No," Stanley heard the father's voice from behind him, "it's from the water. It comes off. See, he's just a man."